Things You've Inherited From Your Mother

Things You've Inherited From Your Mother

by

Hollie Adams

2015 NeWest Press

———

Library and Archives Canada Cataloguing in Publication Adams, Hollie, 1986-, author

Things you've inherited from your mother / Hollie Adams.

(Nunatak first fiction series : 40)

Issued in print and electronic formats.

ISBN 978-1-927063-83-5 (pbk.).--ISBN 978-1-927063-84-2 (epub).-- ISBN 978-1-927063-85-9 (mobi)

I. Title. II. Series: Nunatak first fiction ; 40

PS8601.D4527T45 2015 C813'.6 C2014-906472-1

C2014-906473-X

———

Editor for the Board: Nicole Markotić

Cover and interior design: Vikki Wiercinski @ Half Design

Author photo: Michael G. Khmelnitsky

Cover photo: © HultonArchive / istockphoto.com

NeWest Press acknowledges the support of the Canada Council for the Arts, the Alberta Multimedia Development Fund, and the Edmonton Arts Council for our publishing program. We also acknowledge the financial support of the Government of Canada through the Department of Canadian Heritage (Canada Book Fund).

201, 8540–109 Street Edmonton, Alberta T6G 1E6

780.432.9427

NeWest Press   www.newestpress.com

No bison were harmed in the making of this book.

We are committed to protecting the environment and to the responsible use of natural resources. This book was printed on FSC-certified paper.

1 2 3 4 5 17 16 15 printed and bound in Canada

For my family.

Tuesday your mother died. Ovarian cancer.

Last Tuesday she refused to drink the hospital's coffee-flavoured coffee, asked you to pretty-please drive to that coffee shop with the elaborate coffee that tastes like not-coffee, the coffee that tastes like what rich French people eat for dessert.

"Crème Brûlée would be preferable but I'll settle for Belgian Chocolate." She nodded towards her hospital room door as if to say, "Well, what're you waiting for?"

When you asked her which coffee shop she was talking about, she only made a fluttering motion with her hand, and said, "Oh, you know, any of them that have the good stuff."

You took your time collecting your things from the beside table: a sad-looking wallet, depressed in the middle from a run-in (or run-over) with a car tire (yours); a lid-less ChapStick, the top of which has grown fuzzy from pocket lint; a series of interconnected key-rings linked to a plastic sprinkle donut keychain; a celebrity gossip magazine swiped from the hospital waiting room, the bottom right-hand corner of the cover ripped off to protect the subscriber's anonymity. You moved your body as if swimming in a cream-based soup, lifting your purse slowly to demonstrate what an epic feat of strength it was, saying nothing, because if you gave her some time and made a little show of it, she would suddenly remember her manners, open the top drawer, hand you a bill. A five at least.

But she only added: "Don't forget I'm off dairy. But none of that soy crap either. Lord knows I have enough estrogen coursing through these veins."

You looked to the coat-rack-like apparatus beside her bed, flicked the clear, fluid-filled baggie hanging from it like a giant cartoon raindrop with the nail of your index finger.

"Oh, so that's what's in there. Pure estrogen! Silly doctors. No wonder you're not getting any better." You patted the top of her head, regretting it instantly, fearing her hair, now the consistency of candy floss, would be pushed right off her head by the force of your affection.

"If you would've taken ten minutes out of your busy schedule to read that article I gave you, you'd be off dairy and soy too. Dairy causes cervical cancer. The Swedes have confirmed it."

"And what does soy milk cause? Brain cancer?"

"And bloating." She chin-pointed at your midsection.

"Hey, buddy, my eyes are up here." And you felt glad to be crossing the room towards the door, towards the outside world, even if only to go search the city in rush-hour traffic, hoping you had enough gas to find a mythical cup of non-dairy-non-soy, yet somehow still milked coffee you'd have to charge to your credit card.

Did she believe that if she drank cow's milk now in the throes of one type of terminal cancer, she would also develop another type of terminal cancer? Did she think switching to almond milk would cure her incurable cancer? Or was she just trying to find your limits, test your willingness to help her finish the craft project she's working on from page 29 of *Sewing With Cat Hair*, pushing you until you called her bluff?

How did you deal with her? You must be a saint, a wizard. You should write a book. A how-to self-help manual. For daughters dealing with their impossible dying mothers.

If It Wasn't For The Dying, You Might Kill Your Mother

Imagine: your mother dies. Car accident, pottery class catastrophe, ostrich attack. Or something less sudden. Cancer works. It doesn't really matter what kind, does it? Would one kind be better than another? Maybe. Some are slower, some more masochistic. Probably not skin cancer. Or appendix cancer. Or cancer of the tonsils. Don't imagine those. Pick a vital internal organ between the neck and the pelvis. That type of cancer. Say there was a fair amount of time between the diagnosis and the... passing. Not too much time. A few months. But the diagnosis was terminal, no viable treatment, no Hail-Mary experimental drug. Naturally, you would spend a lot of time with her during these months. First at her home and then the hospital, playing nurse, maid, and, her favourite of the roles, nursemaid. Enough time that you would develop a sore on the inner left of your mouth, the spot you chewed to avoid critiquing the soap operas she insisted *you watch with her, and though she claimed conversation was only allowed during commercial breaks, ensured you received detailed backstories of the characters you couldn't tell apart, explained who was whose estranged father, orphaned daughter, comatose ex-lover, evil pirate-twin, child-prodigy-turned-heroin-addict. Enough time that the sore developed into a hole the width of your top left incisor. Enough time that you felt certain the sore was on the brink of infection by hospital-cafeteria-muffin crumbs. So much time that you might end up wanting to kill her. Figuratively, of course.*

If you do write a book, make sure to mention the time she took out a pair of tiny scissors from her purse and instructed you on the mechanics of cutting the hardened poop pellets out from the matted fur of her cat's bottom because he's too fat to reach back there to lick himself after using the litter box.

"Distract his frontside with a treat first, and stroke his backside with the grain. Go against the grain and you're just asking for trouble," she said, making tiny cuts in the air in front of her face.

Write about her letting him eat Hershey's Kisses and calling his litter box his "potty palace." Write about the shiny balls of foil you later scooped out of the potty palace.

Be sure to mention that her death was her own fault.

Don't let her be the victim in your book. Make sure the reader knows there was a tumour growing somewhere inside her abdomen for years. Years and years. Almost as long as your daughter's been alive. A tumour she adopted as a part of herself, grew familiar with, allowed to settle in and make itself at home.

"Herbie's acting up again," she would say, poking at her left side, encouraging him—it—to sit, stay, roll over, play dead.

Why didn't she have it removed? It used to be a good tumour as far as tumours go: well-trained and lazy, harmless as a Labradoodle. An old dog happy to lie on the mat by the back door, everyone stepping over him to get outside.

"Those doctors would cut your brain out of your head and tell you they were saving your life. I get lumps and bumps all the time, coming and going, an almond here, a golf ball over there. Heck, if Herbie was maldignent, don't you think he'd have finished me off by now?"

If you told her that she means "malignant," she would have asked when you planned to start using that fancy-pants education she paid so much for. "Fancy-pants" her catch-all pejorative adjective.

"I asked for chicken nuggets, not these fancy-pants chicken strips!"

"That fancy-pants plumber is ripping me off again, I know it!"

"Well, look at your fancy-pants shirt! What'd they make that shirt out of? A pair of fancy pants?"

"Maybe Herbie's waiting for the right moment," you offered, "If I were a tumour, I'd try to at least be funny about it, you know, wait for the most comical time to off you, like right after you've made your last mortgage payment."

The woman who named her tumour after an adorable Volkswagen calls you sick and disturbed.

As a procrastinator, your mother took the cake—which she was supposed to take on Monday, but didn't end up taking until the following Wednesday (a grade-A joke you should consider using in your book). She'd get around to it, she'd say. Just like she'd get around to paying her parking tickets, filing her taxes, getting her oil changed. Surgery was just another thing she was putting off, like getting her winter tires changed back over to the all-season ones. And then suddenly it's September and it's almost time to get the winter tires put back on again anyway, so what's the point? Might as well just leave them on now. It'll all straighten itself out in the wash, what's meant to be will be. Que sera sera, and then your car's being impounded by Calgary Parking Services which is fine really because the engine was failing on account of lack of oil. And your mother's dead. Procrastinated herself to death.

You wouldn't say you're also a procrastinator—but you'll get around to saying it one day (too many procrastinator jokes?).

You picture yourself ten years from now, flipping through a book of baby names, trying to decide whether your own tumour is more an Emma or a Sophia. Which is why you are going to the doctor. Soon. Next week. In the very nearish future. Grab the old parking ticket magnetized to the fridge and use its backside to write up a to-do list.

- -

To Do:
— buy cute notepad from expensive stationery store for future to-do lists
— also maybe some pastel-coloured pens?
— write more procrastinator jokes
— pay parking tickets, get oil changed, and/or drive car into river

- -

You may notice that time begins to speed up; the days following your mother's death blur together as if someone has thrown your life and copious amounts of red wine into a blender and hit "liquefy." Naturally, swallowing copious amounts of red wine will counteract this feeling. Other helpful activities include watching reality television and not washing your hair. Replace grocery shopping with picking up fast-food in the drive-thru lane, ordering enough that you can divide it into three square meals, all of which you will eat in the comfort of your unmade bed, using your sheets as napkins.

If you have a type-A older sister, hand her a set of high-lighters and a block of Post-it notes. Watch her take care of every post-mortem detail in under two hours: the obituary for the newspaper; the make, model, and colour of the casket (N.B.: using the word "coffin" will elicit a ten-minute speech from your sister re: empirical evidence that your mother is not a vampire); the prayer for the little card with your mother's face on it (N.B.: do not suggest a monologue from the first season of *The Golden Girls* as a "viable alternative," no matter how beautiful and moving the monologue). The schedule for the visitation, funeral, and wake now wound as tightly as your sister's ballerina bun.

The next morning, open your closet to find a dark grey shirt and pair of dark grey pants adorned with neon "wear me" stickers. A fun thing you could do: show up at the church in the assigned attire with her neon Post-its still affixed to the collar of your blouse and thigh of your pants.

- -

Fact: Post-it notes are available in eight standard sizes, twenty-five shapes, and sixty-two colours.

Fact: Your boss is 64% more likely to give you the day off if you write the request on a Post-it that is pink and flower-shaped.

Do not forget that you have become an orphan. Remind everyone.

Call up your best friend, the one who abandoned you to move to a city more glamourous than Calgary—Montréal, New York, Mexico City, Pensacola. It is late morning, which means early afternoon Florida time—Tina likes to remind you she now lives in the only time zone that really matters.

It has taken all of your energy to get from your bed to the kitchen. Flop the top half of your body onto the counter for support and whine into the phone: "I need you. I have no one else. I'm an orphan."

Because she is your best friend, she will not remind you you're too old to be an orphan—at least in the proper, Dickensian sense—and she won't list off the people in your life who still have a pulse—your daughter, for instance.

Instead she'll offer to come check out prospective orphanages with you.

"Will I have to sleep in a bunk bed?" you ask.

"Oh, yes. On a mattress made of straw."

"Porridge for breakfast, lunch, and dinner?"

"That is the fate of the orphan, I'm afraid," she says.

"And I'll have to sweep the floor with a ratty old broom?" You use your socked feet to sweep last night's dinner crumbs under the oven.

"Well, we couldn't give you a nice, new broom, could we? Next you'd be asking for shoes without holes and an iPhone 6."

"Maybe I'll convince the others to unionize." An entire pepperoni kicked into the void.

"Pip'll never go for it. He thinks unions are basically communism."

As you rinse out the coffee pot, ask if she'll do the honours of leaving you on the front stoop in the middle of the night.

Tina will say something profound: "That is the difference between 'step' and 'stoop,' isn't it? You walk up a step, but you leave an unwanted baby on a stoop."

"Who would stoop so low!" The coffee maker gurgles like a happy baby.

"Imagine if you could still do that," Tina says, "Leave your baby at the hospital or the monastery or wherever. I might have done that with Mitchell. Seriously, if I would have known he'd bite me every time I told him no—I mean really try to take off a chunk of flesh between his teeth—I would've let some nice nuns give him the strap once in a while."

"Are nuns still a thing you can become? You never hear of anyone becoming a nun anymore. It sounds so quaint. Like becoming a cobbler. Or setting up a retirement fund."

"Someone else paying for the diapers and baby food and damage to the neighbour's wading pool, and then when he's got his Mr. Hyde under control—or was Dr. Jekyll the evil one? I can never remember—anyway, when he's lost the taste for human flesh, fate could reunite us. Or Facebook. Of course, nowadays they could track you down, obviously, like with your DNA, but what if monasteries just had to take babies, no questions asked, like they did in the good ol' days? Just leave a little note with his name and whether or not he is gluten intolerant and then you're on your way to the nightclub or—"

"Or off to college," you say, buffing the countertop with your sleeve over your hand.

Silence on Tina's end. Or there would be silence if you couldn't hear Mitchell threatening to disembowel whoever "Baba" is with his teeth.

"Not like I left my mother a note and disappeared in the middle of the night. At least I had the decency to tell her in person she'd be paying for diapers and formula."

You know you're making Tina feel bad, and you're not trying to make her feel bad, but if she does feel bad, she might hop on a plane sooner, stay for longer, a whole week of petting your hair and unwrapping your Reese's Mini Peanut Butter Cups for you.

"Oh, Care, I wasn't talking about you. You did the right thing. Imagine where you'd be working if you hadn't gotten a university degree."

"Most of the people I work with now don't have university degrees."

"But education's important. At least you set a good example for your daughter!"

"You mean getting pregnant in high school, never telling the father, and then leaving the baby with her grandmother while I did keg-stands in my dorm?" You're embellishing— mostly the keg-stands happened in other students' dorms.

"You really should sign Kate up with the Big Sisters program to make sure she has at least one positive female influence in her life," Tina says.

- -

Fact: In order for a "step" to become internationally recognized as a "stoop" it must have been constructed before 1950, be crumbling in either one or both its outer corners, and receive at least one unwanted baby per calendar year.

- -

Self-help books lie. And you don't mean the content of them, though surely some of the content also lies (you say "surely" because you haven't actually ever read a self-help book, though your mother and sister were awfully fond of buying them for you for birthdays and Christmases and Secretary's Day). You mean that the concept of a self-help book written by someone other than yourself is a lie. That someone is not yourself but an expert or doctor or expert doctor. You buy the book, read what someone else tells you to do, do that thing, get healthier/thinner/richer/more psychic and somehow you've helped yourself?

That's like saying that if you go to the cardiologist, have her inspect your heart, prescribe you pills, and then take those pills, you've helped yourself. After all, you took the pills yourself. You didn't need a nurse to shove them in your mouth and rub your throat until you swallowed. But calling that self-medication would be a lie because everyone knows self-medication can only be done with alcohol or non-prescription drugs (or at least not your prescription drugs).

So in order to make your own self-help book less of a lie, you have decided to make the readers do some of the work themselves.

- -

In the space provided, list the problem for which you are seeking self-help:

_____

_____

_____

Which of your parents caused you to develop such a problem?

_____

_____

Which of the following adjectives most accurately describe one or both of your parents? (Circle all that apply):

self-centered • cold
religious-when-convenient • self-righteous
judgmental • cat lover • controlling
owns too many vests • closed-minded
uses coupons

In the space provided, describe the traumatic event from your childhood that has caused you to develop such a problem. Highlight your mother's role in the event.

_____

_____

_____

Ask your mother why she believes you are suffering from this problem and what you should do to remedy the problem. Write her advice below and then rip this section out of the workbook and put it somewhere you'll never have to see it again: the garbage, the shredder, the shoebox in the hall closet marked "Tax Receipts 1990-2000":

_____

_____

Have you tried looking for help on the internet? Write down the three most helpful-sounding pieces of advice you've gained from anonymous forum-posters on the internet:

_____

_____

What do you think you should do to solve your problem?

_____

_____

Try doing that for a while. Write your success story here:

_____

_____

Use the space below to thank the author of this book for solving your problem:

_____

_____

Combating an Unsupportive Support System

Do you have an ex-husband? Surely you do. He is either an accountant or a Grade Two teacher. You met him filing your taxes two months past the deadline or at your daughter's parent-teacher conference, twice rescheduled because you couldn't make the first two dates because you didn't want to.

When you step into his office that is either a carpet-walled cubicle or what looks like the showroom of a crayon factory, and you say, "It's nice to meet you, Mr. Butler," he'll tell you to call him Jerry.

"It's Jerry. Just Jerry is fine."

And you'll make a classic joke like "Well, which do you want to be called? Jerry or Just Jerry?"

And he'll laugh politely and he won't take a seat behind his desk because he is that kind of accountant or Grade Two teacher, the easy-going kind who sits on the edge of the desk instead, the kind who crosses one trousered leg over the other, so that his aggressively patterned sock is now visible under the hem of his right pantleg, and he'll say something like "I'm glad you could make time to come in today, Ms. Fowler," while gesturing towards a blue plastic chair. "Please take a seat."

And then you'll say another profound thing, like "Oh, Carrie is fine."

"Well, okay then, Oh Carrie." The skin around his eyes will crinkle when he smiles.

And that is how to win yourself an ex-husband.

Picture Jerry sitting in his underwear (take the liberty to paint in the tire of flab around his midsection and the grey hair he has inevitably accumulated since your divorce), flipping through the newspaper, stopping at the "Announcements" section, scanning "Deaths," a chocolate chip muffin unceremoniously un-topped in one bite. The name of his ex-mother-in-law in bold type beneath a picture of her in her thirties (one of her many dying wishes), wrinkle-free and auburn-beehived. He drops a cup of boiling coffee on his crotch, his "Over the Hill" mug shattering on the tile floor as he chokes on chocolate chips.

Except, if he were in the daily habit of skimming the paper for deceased ex-relatives, he certainly would have called by now to offer his condolences. He may want to scoop out your eyeballs with scalding soup ladles, but surely he has enough decency to extend bereavement sympathies.

Which means he hasn't found out. You could call but your last attempt at a serious phone conversation with Jerry drove you to rent *You've Got Mail* and down a shot of tequila every time either character wrote an email. The scene in which they begin instant messaging one another was particularly demanding and you're just not sure you're up for that kind of commitment.

Kate had no interest in the movie but eventually abandoned her homework in the dining room, joined you on the couch, begged you to let her lick salt off the back of her hand too. So you got her her own shotglass—hoped she wouldn't read the cursive neon writing and ask you about the words "spring break 2001"—and poured her some lemonade.

You'd yell "Drink!" and she'd copy the way you'd lick the salt, throw your head back, swallow with your eyes closed. She'd mimic your pucker, her tongue sticking out in pretend disgust. Her eyes only half on the movie, she drowned out Tom Hanks's quippy backhanded compliments with her gleeful cries of "Drink! Drink!" As soon as you finished your shots, she'd be ready to go again. Kate not following the rules, the game for her had nothing to do with the movie, nothing to do with ex-husbands.

Then you, approaching 2001-spring-break-level intoxication, and Kate, crazed on a sugar rush, both pretend to be Rockettes, cancanning around the coffee table, all jazz hands and high-kicks. Kate ruins the moment by pointing out how mad Jerry is going to be if he finds out you were dancing on the coffee table and when is he coming over?

Do not go looking for a bottle of tequila, do not see if *You've Got Mail* is available to stream on Netflix. Do not call to Kate upstairs to ask if she remembers how to play "Shots With Mommy."

You're better than that now. You're a sophisticated grown-up who just yesterday bought two bottles of Pinot Noir on sale at Grape Expectations. It is 10:56. If you recently promised yourself you would stop drinking before lunchtime, pop a frozen breakfast burrito into the microwave for good measure.

*

When you do write your own how-to self-help manual, consider making it one of those "Choose Your Own Adventure" books Kate used to read before her body was invaded by a Sylvia-Plath-craving parasite with a smart mouth and an unquenchable taste for organic kale.

You stumbled upon one such book in the basement last evening, busying yourself reorganizing boxes of things you've been meaning to get rid of: Jerry's bowling trophies; your mother's hand-me-down cookbooks with her notes in the margins ("when the directions say 'oven,' Carrie, they mean your *real* oven, the big metal thing with the four black swirlies on top—not your microwave oven); your CD collection which sadly has accrued no resale value despite your insistence that a box-set of John Hughes movie soundtracks was a good investment; a box of clothes for each of Kate's fashion eras—her magenta period, her animal-print phase, and that inexplicable period when hospital scrubs were a popular everyday fashion choice at Kate's school and she came home every evening like a harried child prodigy just out of surgery.

Wouldn't human existence be exponentially easier if for every scenario, a set of words would flash before your eyes offering you just two choices? A fifty-fifty chance to do the right thing, every time.

You could offer such choices to your readers: "Upgrade Mom to private hospital suite, turn to page 16" or "Leave Mom in generic shared room with visibly unstable former bus driver who claims the government injected her with neurosyphilis, turn to page 47." On page 16 your mother is forgiving you for getting pregnant in high school (let it be known, you did not *have* the baby in high school. Your daughter was delivered well after your high school graduation. And because this was a time before you had to, by law, publish all life events on every platform of social media, most of the people you went to high school with don't even know you got pregnant. Including the guy who convinced you the condom was already on). And then over on page 47, you find yourself cut out of the will. Only two options. No grey areas. No other choices. It wouldn't even be possible to be tempted by other options like "Try to convince Izzy it would be in both your best interests if she converted her living room into a home hospice and hired a private care nurse" or "Flirt tirelessly with mother's rat-faced doctor only to find out weeks later he has absolutely nothing to do with room assignments."

Give your book a catchy title: *Putting the "Can" Back in "Cancer."* Don't mention anywhere on the cover it's a Choose-Your-Own-Adventure so your readers don't have to be embarrassed when the woman sitting next to them on the C-Train leans over to ask whether they are enjoying their "little activity book."

They won't have to say, "Yes, the cover indicates the intended audience is a youth of approximately six to twelve years of age, but the puzzles in this issue of *Highlights Magazine* are actually quite challenging."

Instead they can lower their eyes and flash their cover of *Finding the Humour in Your Tumour* and solemnly tell that woman with the neck scarf tied in what looks like an expert sailor's knot, "I'm reading it for my mother. Cancer. Stage five," and when she says she thought there were only four stages of cancer, your readers can say, "According to the latest research, stage five is the elaborate funeral your narcissistic mother has planned for herself—pre-death and actually pre-diagnosis—because she can't bear the thought of not being alive and the centre of attention when all her friends and family are crying over her and fawning over her and telling their most flattering stories about her." Your readers can wipe tears from their eyes and tell that woman, "This is the only book that really gets it. By Carrie Fowler. Look at her author photo. It must be Photoshopped, don't you think? No one can be this good-looking *and* this intelligent."

- -

To-Do List:
— get Kate to take your photo before you age another day (does Ben have Photoshop on laptop?)
— return *Putting the "Can" Back in "Cancer"* and *Finding the Humour in Your Tumour* back to library (attempt to read another chapter? already overdue?)

- -

*

Start your book with a joke. Something like, "Why can nervous people never be good in a symphony orchestra? Because they'd lose their composer." But funnier and more relevant.

*

What will you eat for breakfast? *Choose toast and flip to page 81 or Take the cereal and skip to page 112.*

   You choose to eat both toast and cereal which is the equivalent of flipping to both page 81 and 112 to see which of the two might feature your untimely free-fall down an empty elevator shaft. That's the problem with those books: they invite you to cheat the system. Unfortunately, you cannot both call Jerry and not call Jerry. Rest the phone back in its cradle, return to your carbohydrates and caffeine.

The newspaper is sitting on the counter where Ben left it, out of order, folded the wrong way on its seams. Begin your morning paper-reading ritual: read every single one of the headlines in the front section and every first paragraph of the articles in the World News section. Amid alternating bites of real toast and simulated-cinnamon-toast-flavoured cereal, you learn the first case of Ebola was diagnosed in the United States, a Spanish cave explorer has been rescued after being trapped for twelve days, and "Creeky," the world's oldest clown, is dead at ninety-eight. You will now spend the day trying to work these three subjects into conversation. Preferably the same conversation.

For dessert, pour yourself another bowl of cereal and a glass of wine (hey, it's almost noon and your mother is dead).

You are making significant progress un-encrypting the Cryptoquote (you either have every letter completely right or absolutely none of them) when the phone rings. The mouthful of red wine that was halfway down your throat is now on your pajama top which is, of course, white. If your current partner refuses to sleep with you at the moment because "it's just too soon" after your mother's death, the shape of the stain will remind you of a hand reaching to undo the buttons on your pajama top.

Answer the phone hesitantly, sure you've telepathically summoned Jerry's sympathy.

"Carrie, do you think there'll be enough flowers?" Your sister's been calling so frequently you'd swear you were a radio station giving away free tickets to see her favourite lecturer debate the merits of stem cell research.

"Hi, Izzy."

"I keep calling the florist who's assured me there will be plenty, but I want it to look really nice, you know? Not just thrown together at the last second like we didn't put any thought into it." Immediate action is clearly called for. You must take preventative measures: wet a dishcloth and begin patting at the wine stain.

"Right, you want people to think we've been planning Mom's funeral for some time now. Like while she was lying on her deathbed vomiting out her insides, asking us to suffocate her with her too-flat pillow—just like that Spanish cave explorer who was trapped for twelve days before they rescued him—we were thinking about the placement of the petunias."

"Don't be ridiculous, Carrie. Petunias are *not* funeral flowers."

Your sister has no comment about the cave explorer and instead launches into a diatribe about flower placement in terms of size and colour. If red roses are placed next to pink ones, it will look like the red is bleeding into the pink. Apparently a bad thing.

"I didn't know lesbians were flower experts. Isn't that gay man territory? I'm pretty sure you're stepping on some toes here. Speaking of stepping on toes, I bet clowns get their toes stepped on a lot. You know because of their huge feet, which reminds me that today—"

"Don't be stupid. It makes the red less vibrant and makes pink look like a second-rate colour. Ideally, they would be separated by white carnations and the arrangements need to be symmetrical, obviously, on both sides of the casket." You succeed in changing the red stain to a larger, second-rate pink one.

"Well *obviously*," you say, "but I bet you anything Mom won't notice. You know what she would've loved, though? If Poncho came to the funeral. You know she liked him more than the two of us combined. And we can get him one of those kitty-cat tuxedos with a hole at the back for his tail." Poncho glowers at you from the countertop, narrowing his black marbly eyes in a way that directly translates to "I'd rather have Ebola."

"Thanks for taking this seriously, Care. See you at the funeral home tonight. Please don't be late. Seriously. If I have to stand alone up there and shake all those hands myself— And what are you doing over there? Playing with velcro? It's so loud, my—"

"Oh, I'm sorry for chewing my breakfast, maybe you should learn not to call during mealtimes! Whatever happened to manners and etiquette?" you ask, mouth full of tiny cinnamon toasts, milk dribbling onto your chin.

"Wear the grey outfit. I put a green Post-it on it. And don't leave the sticky on to spite me." Perhaps you underestimated Izzy.

"Oh, I would never! Grey and green don't even go together."

"Oh, and I called Jerry because I knew you wouldn't."

She hangs up before you can sputter toast-flavoured-toast into the mouthpiece. You would call her ex, Samantha, and invite her along to this shindig—Izzy thinks monogamy is "patriarchal" and trading women like baseball cards is "feminist"—but she also thinks not introducing you to her girlfriends is "common sense" so you don't actually have Samantha's number. Or a clear picture in your head of what she looks like. Or any basic information about her including age, last name, or country of residence.

Poncho stretches his fat cat belly on the kitchen cutting board. He licks his nose while maintaining eye contact. Definitely a threat of some sort. You wonder when you last washed the cutting board. You also wonder whether cat dander is edible; it's unlikely you'll remember to wash the cutting board whenever it is you cook next (i.e., weeks from now).

You dump your toasted crusts into the garbage bin under the sink. No, "dump" is the wrong word since it implies a sort of falling from your plate down into the bin, and since the garbage is on the brink of overflowing, the phrase "balance your crusts precariously on a veritable hill of decomposing waste" seems more apropos. Despite your best attempts, one of your crusts teeters and falls to the linoleum. Your family follows the Jenga rule of garbage duty, meaning it's your turn to take out the trash. You grab the bag by its four corner flaps and heave it out of its cylindrical holding cell to discover the no-name brand bag has sprung a leak, a fountain of tuna juice.

"C'mon, be a good boy and lap this up so Mommy doesn't have to get out the mop."

Poncho raises himself off the cutting board, dismounts the countertop by way of the kitchen table, and ambles away in the opposite direction.

"What, are you broken? Is it the smell of your favourite food that's driving you away?" You toss your wine-stained dishcloth at him. Too lazy to flinch as it lands on the arch of his back, he wears it like a saddle into the living room.

- -

Things You've Inherited From Your Mother

1. One purple '91 Buick Regal that smells of sun-baked beef jerky and deceased buttermilk; namely, that smells of your mother's cat Poncho, whose dietary mainstays included excessive amounts of beef jerky, gourmet pesto-flavoured tuna, and buttermilk. (You never succeeded in convincing your mother that contrary to adorable cartoons from the 1950s, cats shouldn't actually drink milk.) Poncho always rode shotgun in the Buick, regardless of whether there were four other non-feline passengers aboard. May it be known that you are as much a cat person as you are a Buick Regal person.

2. One half of your mother's one-storey house in Airdrie, Alberta that is charming in the way aluminum fences and green shingles are charming. Ginger fur blanketing every surface not wrapped in plastic furniture covers. A basement with liquor-store boxes, all unlabeled and uncategorized, so you have to empty and sort through each one before you can know for certain that you will end up just throwing everything away. Scratched walls and doors with measurements written on them, though the ticks run horizontally rather than vertically—not a chart of yours and Izzy's growth but of Poncho's. You can't believe your mother ever had the nerve to criticize your house for "smelling like the smoking section of a Waffle House."

3. One wardrobe of elastic-waist jeans, vests with sewn-on appliqués themed after every holiday from Christmas to Remembrance Day, and a septuplet set of faux-leather loafers. You find the outfits you and your sister bought her (or rather, your sister bought and you were forced to fork over money for some time after the fact because she didn't think a will-writing kit was ever an appropriate birthday present) in a cardboard box in the basement marked "Goodwill."

4. One morbidly obese tabby cat who has been both haughty and melodramatic since your mother died, whom you've inherited as a means of "converting" your "heathen ways" because you once mentioned to her that you were, if anything, more of a dog person. When you told Izzy you would graciously forfeit your custody of Poncho, she threatened to take you to court.

- -

The phone rings again as you near the midway-point of your bottle of wine.

"Got it!" Kate calls from the other end of the house. Good, you think, let her deal with Izzy and the placement of the petunias. Although it might really be Jerry this time—or another telemarketer.

You quite enjoyed taking a call from a telemarketer earlier this morning, feigning confusion ("Auntie Claire? Is that you?"), not waiting for a response before sobbing into the receiver, rambling on about not getting to say goodbye ("It all happened so fast... I thought I'd have more time!") while the bewildered cold-caller went from trying to peddle a low-interest credit card to trying to eject herself from the conversation as tactfully as possible. ("Perhaps I called at a bad time... Please don't really hang yourself from the ceiling fan if I hang up.")

- -

Pie Chart of the Types of People Who Call Your Landline Now That Your Mother Is Dead

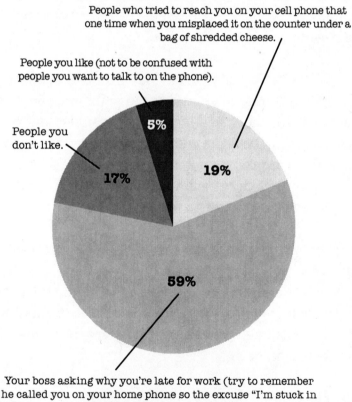

People who tried to reach you on your cell phone that one time when you misplaced it on the counter under a bag of shredded cheese.

People you like (not to be confused with people you want to talk to on the phone).

People you don't like.

5%

17%

19%

59%

Your boss asking why you're late for work (try to remember he called you on your home phone so the excuse "I'm stuck in traffic" won't work probably)

- -

Kate wanders into the kitchen, cradling the cordless phone between her ear and shoulder, swirling a glass of water in one hand, the ice cubes tink-tinking against the glass. Her eyes are red behind the non-prescription tortoiseshell glasses she wears to look "sophisticated," but at least half her mouth is smiling.

"Who is it?" you ask in a loud whisper. She makes a swatting motion with her free hand.

"I'm doing okay, I guess. Thanks for asking," she says into the receiver. "The funeral's on Friday. I'd really like it if you could come." Who told Kate she could go around inviting people like it's her Sweet Sixteen? You already threw her one of those. Against her will. Unicorn-themed.

She opens the refrigerator and rummages through the crisper.

"I know it might be a little awkward to be around the whole family, but—"

You creep around behind her and lean towards the phone. A male voice. Male words you can't quite make out.

"Ooh, a boy!" you shriek. "Is it your new boyfriend?"

Earlier that week you listened in on a call between Kate and her best friend Andrea, a name Kate insists you pronounce with emphasis on the second syllable. Apparently Kate's in the early stages of a relationship with someone called "Branson." Apparently he is "so handsome he could be British."

You've been meaning to steal her cellphone to find out if there's been any "sexting" going on. You saw quite an eye-opening special about it on *Dateline NBC*. Apparently, the kids are really into sending each other naked photos of themselves because they know their fellow teens to be so trustworthy and respectful that they would never share such compromising photos with their friends or post them on the internet where they will be looked at for eternity by classmates, strangers, and whatever species outlives humans and learns how to use search engines.

Kate whirls around and leaves the fridge empty-handed to hunker into the pantry. You wonder when you last saw her eat something that wasn't a raw vegetable. You hear her apologize to her gentleman caller more politely than she has ever spoken to you. Ever.

Position yourself outside the pantry door. Fueled by almost a bottle of Pinot Noir, begin making the most obnoxious kissing noises you can muster, in between verses of a new song you've composed called "Katie-Kate's in Love." The song takes a sad turn when the only word you can rhyme with "boyfriend" is "end."

Kate's head pokes out of the pantry, gives you her best "you're ruining my life" look: a cross between looking directly into sunlight and sucking on a lemon. "Mother, seriously, shut up." Kate has taken to calling you "Mother" recently. She says it in such a way that you get the feeling she'd like to add another word after "Mother." You've been meaning to begin calling her "Katrina" in response, but it's always too many syllables.

- -

A conversation you love having:
Stranger: Katrina, like the hurricane?
Possible Answer #1: Yes, when I was pregnant in the year 1999, I predicted there would be a terrible hurricane named Katrina six years later that would

devastate the southeastern United States, and I decided it would make a beautiful namesake for my daughter.

Possible Answer #2: If you mean has she also killed 1,800 people and been responsible for $100 billion in damage, then yes, just like the hurricane.

Possible Answer #3: No, it's pronounced "Katrina" like the eastern European stripper name.

- -

Still in sing-song, you taunt her for being embarrassed.

"Someone's blushing! Am I embarrassing you? I'd hate to embarrass you in front of your new boyfriend."

Kate covers one end of the receiver with her palm.

"Yes. I am. Embarrassed for you. You know who's on the phone with me right now? It's Jerry, and he can hear you acting like a five-year-old."

You have always supported Kate's continued relationship with Jerry even after your relationship with him dissolved, and by "dissolved" you of course mean "he decided to start cheating on you with the gym teacher."

"Oh. Well, tell him I said hello. Very nice of him to call."

Return to your wine, finish the bottle in three quick gulps.

Being a responsible mother, check to see if Kate has eaten today.

Being a smart-ass daughter, Kate will check to see if you've been grocery shopping this month.

"Everything in the fridge is spoiled."

"Well maybe you should stop buying it every toy it asks for."

"I touched a potato in the bread drawer that was totally soft."

"You know the rules, Kate. You touch it, you eat it."

*

Wake sometime later that evening on the couch, legs dangling over the armrest. You wish you'd had the sense to dispose of the evidence: the empty wine bottle lies on the coffee table across the sympathy-card-turned-coaster your boss mailed you, all your coworkers' names signed in the same handwriting. Luckily you never got dressed that morning so you were able to sleep comfortably in your wine-stained pajamas.

From the couch you can see into the dining room where Ben sits hunched at the table marking papers on top of a *National Geographic* to avoid scratching the wood. His reading glasses balance on the tip of his nose, making him look older than... How old is he now? Thirty-six? That must be it; he just had a birthday when? Shit, when's his birthday? This week?

- -

Things to Do
—steal Ben's driver's license when he's in the shower
—see what else in wallet? (isn't his money your money at this point?)
—buy birthday present (something you'll both enjoy, like tickets to Stars on Ice or the new set of bedsheets you've been meaning to buy)
—if already missed birthday, plan surprise party for next weekend, insist "pretending to forget" his birthday all part of elaborate plan

—choose theme for surprise birthday party (something you'll both enjoy, like roller disco)

- -

"Morning, Sunshine," he says without looking up.

You catch your reflection in the black, blank screen of the television. You are the spitting image of a cockatiel coming off hard drugs.

"Oh, I wasn't really sleeping. Just resting my eyes," you say. Furiously try to rub away the sleep collected in their corners.

"Care, you've been passed out since I got home. Two hours ago. And you've been talking in your sleep. Mumbling vulgarities at the cat, actually. I'm sure he would appreciate an apology." Ben still hasn't looked up from his numbers, not missed a beat checking and x-ing.

"In my defense, I drank a bit too much wine and passed out."

"That's not a defense. That's just a literal description of what you did."

"Why didn't you wake me?" You continue attempting to preen yourself in the television screen, trying to untangle what was once your hair and is now a cozy nesting place for small to medium-sized woodland creatures.

"I tried," he says, "You almost bit off my hand." The monotone of Ben's voice is so soothing.

"Oh. Hm. I see. Speaking of food, what do you want for dinner?"

"How about chicken?"

"Damn. I was hoping you'd say dirty dishes."

*

Your mother met Ben during one of her surprise visits to the city. She let herself in through your unlocked backdoor, found Ben dusting the bookshelf in the living room, and assumed you had hired a cleaning service.

"Does your company hire many of you men?" she asked him. "In my day you wouldn't hear of such a thing, but if women can be garbage collectors and cab drivers, I guess there's nothing stopping you."

Despite such auspicious beginnings, you mother quite liked Ben, which she made clear by repeatedly saying she thought he was "good for you" and "just what you needed." You often responded with some variant of "Yes, I have no idea how the fish survived without its bicycle," to which she replied with some variant of "That fish had better strap itself to that bicycle and hold on for dear life before some younger, flashier-coloured fish comes along."

Since meeting her, Ben refuses to engage in any sort of meaningful conversation regarding your mother and will only respond to your complaints with the refrain "She means well." It is his worst quality.

- -

Things You Adore Most About Ben

1. He is not Jerry.

2. When you face monumental challenges to which you can see no feasible solution he dreams up elaborate plans you never thought could work, such as pausing the movie to drive to the store to buy a new bag of salt and vinegar chips.

3. Ben does not judge you for what you do for a living (possibly because he isn't completely sure), your past relationships, your parenting techniques, your red-wine intake, your repeated failures to quit smoking ...

4. He knows how to make you fall asleep fast on restless nights. You only have to ask him about his day and he will dutifully drone on about the politics of college administration and his displeasure at the inexplicable fact that none of his students are as enthusiastic about theories and proofs as he was in college.

5. The man knows his way around a kitchen. You've never once seen him bump into a fridge or an oven.

6. He is so thin you can feel the ribs in his back, which until now you had totally forgotten were a part of a human anatomy; his eyesight is so bad he needs to wear glasses that reverse-magnify (is there a proper word for this?) his eyes to the point that it is hard to tell what colour they are; and anyone who thinks the human body is symmetrical has never seen the guy's back hair (Wait—what was this list about, again?)

— —

3

How to Get Back on That Horse After Your Mother Passes and Convince Your Partner to Jump Your Bones

1. Prepare: don't wash your hair—have you heard of phero-mones?—or shave any part of your body. Shaving suggests you planned for this. Everyone knows spontaneity breeds sexy. Plus you forgot to pick up new blades for your razor and the dull, rusted one you've been using for a month now removes hair with the efficiency of a cheese grater.

2. Make sure you have the house to yourselves: talk up the virtue of the slumber party to your daughter. When she inevitably asks if An-DREY-uh can spend the night, blank on a good excuse, relent, order them a pizza, and aim to get back on that horse next weekend.

3. Wear something sexy, but not brand-new lingerie—again, not spontaneous, suggests you're trying too hard. Although, lingerie he's already seen defeats the whole purpose of lingerie: gone is the element of surprise and novelty. A pair of underwear that does not have any holes, or at least any noticeable holes—the lighting will be dim, after all—the waist of which is at least three finger lengths below your belly button, will certainly be a surprise. No clean underwear fitting this description? No problem! Skip the underwear and just wear a long t-shirt. Instant negligee. Though he may mistake this as pajamas. "You're tired too? Good, I was just thinking how ready for bed I am," he will say and then fall asleep in fewer than four minutes.

4. Speaking of lighting: turn off the harsh, bright overhead light and for lack of candles, turn on only the reading lamp on the nightstand. "Perfect," he says after he crawls into bed and begins to undress a biography of Winston Churchill from its dust jacket.

5. Pour some wine: drink two glasses while watching reruns of *Law & Order*. Fall asleep on the couch.

6. Play some mood music: smooth jazz, R&B, mellow rock music even—any of these will put him in the mood to ask you to turn off the music—he's trying to read.

7. Throw caution to the slight wind generated by your humidifier: remove all your clothes (yes, even your slippers)—you could do this in a striptease fashion but he's reading so you might as well save your energy—straddle

him, take the book from his hands (do not lose his place when you set his book on the nightstand or the moment will be ruined), kiss his neck, suck gently on his earlobe—"Carrie, what are you doing?" he will ask as if you're performing a shocking and unfamiliar action, like flossing.

"Well, I'm not trying to show you a cool, new breakdance move."

"I just don't think ... You're in a very vulnerable state right now."

"Yeah, this straddle position really makes the old thighs burn. I probably should've stretched first."

"I meant your mother—"

"And that's a wrap, ladies and gentlemen!"

*

The morning of the funeral, another of Izzy's outfit choices bleats at you from the full-length bathroom mirror when you realize that this will be the first time you'll see Jerry in months and you look like an L.L. Bean catalogue model. What if getting divorced from you was the impetus he needed to regain his youth? As the jilted lover, you deserve some sort of revenge.

Check the back of your closet. Surely there is a box of clothes back there you had enough insight to save from college (a time when choosing an outfit was not determined by what might remain comfortable should you choose to catch a nap on your lunch break). Inevitably, there will be only one black item in the box: a figure-flattering skirt that falls just above the knee. Funeral perfect. It is a little tight going on but zips up almost all the way. Your shirt will cover the exposed bit of back flab you've been calling your lumbar loaf. If only that flap of skin had a zipper, you'd never have to carry a purse.

Kate eyebrows your outfit as you climb into the car. It's been ages since she saw you look this good. You'll have to hide this skirt when you get home so she doesn't pilfer it.

Once in the church, your sister gets one look at you, mouths the words "Oh Maggot," and drags you by the elbow into the bathroom.

"Oh my God," she says once you're alone, forcing you to face facts: your lip-reading skills may be lacking.

"Have you just been overcome by the holy spirit?" you ask, digging in your purse for lipstick.

"A skintight *leather* skirt? What happened to the outfit I picked out for you?" She paces the length of the stalls, click-clacking her heels on the white and blue ceramic.

"Poncho mistook it for an ugly outfit and peed on it."

"And the fishnet nylons?"

"Every other pair had runs in them?" you offer.

"So you thought, 'A million little holes is better than one run?' You look like *Pretty Woman*."

"Thank you."

"I didn't mean a pretty woman. I meant Julia Roberts in *Pretty Woman*. Pre-Richard Gere. Minus the good hair."

"Well, I dunno, Iz. The title does have the word 'pretty' in it."

"And here I thought the worst fashion crisis I had to deal with was Mom. Can you believe she wanted to be buried in a jumpsuit? You are totally your mother's daughter."

"You take that back!"

If you stand on your tiptoes in front of the mirror above the sink, you can see your outfit to your knees. In the harsh fluorescent light you realize the look on Kate's face might not have been one of adoration, or your next guess, jealousy.

Reluctantly take your place next to Ben. Shake hands with people you don't recognize as they tell you how sorry they are. Notice the corners of their mouths curling when their eyes pan down to your lower half.

"Too bad I left my leather chaps at home," quips one of your mother's friends.

Tell him your mother specifically requested an '80s -themed funeral. Poke his chest with your index finger for emphasis.

"You, sir, are the one whose outfit is inappropriate." You don't think you'll have to talk to him again.

Had your mother thought of it before she died, she may actually have requested a themed funeral, and it might very well have been the '80s. Or Tiki. Or Christmas in July. Or Murder Mystery.

"Why didn't you tell me to change before we left the house?" you hiss in Ben's ear.

He shrugs. "You look... well, kind of hot, actually." You have only heard Ben use the word "hot" in reference to things like stolen goods or the Sahara Desert. He usually saves a lesser adjective to compliment you, like "breath-taking" or "the most beautiful woman he has ever seen."

You say the word "hot" in your head. "Hot, hot, hot" and you are ready to strut your stuff down the centre aisle like it is your own personal catwalk. The choruses to several '80s pop songs begin playing on shuffle from a boom-box you envision the minister carrying on his shoulder. You consider stopping in the middle of the church to vogue à *la* Madonna, when you see Jerry sitting in a middle pew: sans grey hair, sans spare tire.

Your strutting turns into awkward sidesteps as you try to distance yourself a little ways from Ben; pick up your pace without making it too obvious, so that maybe Jerry won't notice that the two of you are together. Maybe he will think Ben is the secret half-brother your family kept locked in the basement, only allowed to see daylight in dire circumstances such as the death of his mother. However, Ben increases his pace accordingly until the two of you are in an almost footrace to overtake the priest. Tina gives you a thumbs-up from the second pew, which seems totally inappropriate, but you appreciate the gesture. You *are* doing a very good job of not tripping.

Then it dawns on you that Kate's definitely told Jerry about Ben, even though she refuses to tell you her home-room teacher's name or what the lunch special was at the school cafeteria on Friday. You're feeling as open as the registration book that was in the funeral parlour for the past two days, a book that you didn't know whether you, as the daughter, were supposed to sign.

Also sitting alone is Howie from work, wearing an ill-fitting sportcoat over a T-shirt with the outline of a tuxedo printed on it. When you make eye contact with him he puts both hands over where his heart would be if he weren't a vacuous shell of chauvinism. A cigarette would make everything approximately infinite times better.

Find your seat in the reserved row at the front of the church. You don't recall ever sitting in a "reserved row" and for a moment you feel like you've won a prize. Then the organ music quiets so everyone can hear your leather skirt squeak across the wooden pew. You now notice the skirt is perhaps not real leather (there was that two-week vegan phase in college) and you have to release the zipper another inch in order to sit down, your muffin top springing geyser-like from the waistband. Crossing your legs, however, remains an impossible feat. To distract yourself from the inability to sufficiently inhale, mentally recite the chorus of Madonna's "Like a Prayer." Funeral perfect.

Next to you, Izzy appears to be in a staring contest with your dead mother lying in her casket, now a figure from a wax museum, an exhibit on business women from decades past. You try to decide whether she resembles Gertrude Stein or seventh-marriage Elizabeth Taylor.

"I can't believe Mom wanted to be buried with her eyes open," you whisper. "We shouldn't have let her have that one."

Your inner thighs, bloated salmon fighting against their fishnets, grow uncomfortably moist. The leather skirt, much like yourself at the moment, is not breathing properly.

"She looks so peaceful," Izzy whispers back.

"She looks like she just walked into her surprise welcome party in heaven."

The priest's eulogy contains many generic adjectives— "giving," "sympathetic," "selfless," "humble,"— which probably apply to most dead people, but betray the fact that he didn't really know your mother. For most of the eulogy you busy yourself trying out different sitting positions within your very limited range of motion in an attempt to find one which doesn't make you feel like a sleeping bag being shoved into an impossibly small nylon sac. Every time you change positions your skirt audibly chafes against the pew like a wet balloon. Then the priest commands, "All rise." Only one appropriate response: a resounding "AMEN!" Except no one else echoes your sentiments. A hundred eyes burning into the back of your head, everyone asking themselves who let Izzy's secret half-sister out of the basement... Izzy's secret half-sister who hasn't seen the light of day since the height of Madonna's musical career.

Immediately after the funeral you will be herded down into the church basement for the wake. The basement will remind you of the inside of your elementary school gymnasium with a lower ceiling. You will wish you were playing a game of dodgeball. Try to avoid hitting people with spherical items from deep inside your purse.

Tina, wearing a Kentucky Derby-sized black hat, tells you it was a beautiful service.

"*Was* it beautiful? Everyone keeps saying that, but I can't tell if they're lying. I think I blacked out from lack of oxygen," you say, looting a butter tart of its raisins.

"No, honestly, it wasn't really that beautiful, I don't know why I said that." Tina reaches into her purse and half-withdraws something metal and flask-shaped.

"This is my mother's funeral! We are in a house of God! I can't believe I didn't think to bring booze. What the hell was I thinking? I wasn't thinking, that's what. Where is the nearest bathroom?" You swipe her flask and head upstairs.

*

When you return to the basement three shots of Fireball later, Izzy is holding a styrofoam cup in one hand and swirling a plastic ladle in the punch bowl with her other hand.

Tina, who has always been terrified of your sister, makes a beeline for the honey-glazed ham (pun intended). You like to joke that Tina is a homophobe, but really she's only phobic of your sister. And for good reason.

During Izzy's first babysitting job for the two of you, she asked if you wanted to play "hostage." You happily agreed, following her to the basement where she tied you both to chairs using skipping ropes. It actually was a pretty fun game for about thirty seconds and then she duct-taped your father's dirty socks into your mouths, shut off the lights, and left you in the dark basement for over two hours. You could hear her and her friends upstairs practicing the dance moves to "Thriller," Izzy laughing, offering scoops of ice cream, doing her best impersonation of a non-sociopath. In order to keep you quiet, Izzy threatened that if any of your parents found out, Tina's Yorkie Porkchop would mysteriously "go missing."

*

"Where have you been? Everyone's been asking about you." Izzy ladles out a scoop of punch and then instead of filling her cup, she lets it slowly drip back into the bowl.

"I had to teach an altar boy about the divine secrets of the Ya-Ya Sisterhood."

"Please stop calling your vulva that."

If she asks if there's whisky on your breath, assure her it's of the holy variety.

"What most people don't know is that after Jesus changed the water into wine, he changed cinnamon hearts into Fireball Whisky."

"How can you be so insensitive?"

"About Christianity?"

Izzy smacks the ladle into the punch, sending fruit cocktail splattering onto her cheekbones. She begins to sniffle. You try to contain it. Comfort her with a soothing speech of "There, there, Sister Dear, there, there" with a hand on her bicep.

"Jesus, Iz, your arms are as hard as well-defined muscles!" For some reason this has the effect of escalating her sniffling into full-blown weeping.

Grab Ben by the tweed-patched elbow.

"Ben, help. Izzy's lost it." Ben is in the process of decimating a powdered-sugar doughnut. His beard has experienced a snowfall of roughly two centimetres.

"Sure, Care. Let's see... Her mother died and she's upset. Yeah, we should have her committed."

"I love how on the same page we are. Quick, what number am I thinking of between one and three thousand?"

"Trick question. You hate numbers and refuse to think about them."

*

You steer Izzy towards your mother's two sisters, whom you have mentally nicknamed "Epidemic" and "The Plague," as you only see either of them at funerals. You leave Izzy with a Kleenex you were keeping in your bra along with fifty others and head outside to light up. As you reach the door it flies open hitting you hard in the nose. Jerry. Of course. Try to lighten the mood with a funny joke like: "Don't worry everyone, I got used to this sort of abuse while we were married!"

"Carrie, listen, I am so sorry." Surprisingly, he doesn't have his eyes trained on the ceiling like he usually does when he's lying.

"It's fine... I don't think it's broken," you say, putting a hand to your nose to check for blood.

"Oh, uh, no, I mean about your mother. Well, the door, too, but I mean—Are you okay?"

"Yeah, no blood or anything."

"Sorry?" He seems genuinely confused. You forgot his synapses fired in slow motion.

Speak slower this time: "I don't think you deviated my septum, but if I do have to have a nose job, I'm asking for the Jennifer Aniston and sending you the bill."

"No, I mean are you okay? Your mom... Oh, Carrie." Jerry tilts his head, steps closer, reaches a hand toward you. You extend both your arms into hug position, but he changes his mind and pats your forearm instead.

"If you need anything," he says, and steps past you before you can ask for a double gin and tonic.

Refocus. The cigarette will have to wait. Ben and Jerry must be kept on opposite sides of the basement. Jerry has made his way over to Kate and Tina. You send the two of them telepathic messages not to let him out of their sight. You find Ben at the buffet table and grab him by the hand.

"Look, I of all people can appreciate a dish composed almost entirely of potatoes and mayonnaise that still has the guts to throw caution to the wind and call itself a salad, but my sister needs us."

"We haven't had food in the house all week." He frowns longingly into the Tupperware bowl.

"Oh right, I forgot you legally weren't allowed inside a grocery store."

You position Ben on Izzy's left side and you take the right. Begin consoling her with newfound vigour.

"At least she's not in pain anymore," you say, a handy phrase you picked up at the funeral parlour where approximately every single person there offered it to you.

"Okay, but now I am in pain. Take it easy, Care, you're rubbing pills into my cashmere."

"If I had pills, you better believe I wouldn't be wasting them on your sweater."

Ben just stands there with his hands in his pockets, not rubbing Izzy's arms, not offering sympathetic phrases. No help at all.

Izzy, however, appears to be in much better spirits since Jerry arrived, which can only mean she takes pleasure watching you handle your own personal apocalypse and thanking her lucky stars she doesn't believe in monogamous relationships or copulating with Y-chromosome mammals.

Cigarettes form a conga line in your brain. You notice Kate has abandoned her post and moved into the far corner to link arms with that Andrea girl, whom she needed to bring for "moral support." How could she have gotten so distracted? You shouldn't have counted on her.

At least Tina still has Jerry occupied. You watch her give one of his inane jokes a convincing fake-laugh while she packs up desserts into napkins and sneaks them into her purse. Cough loudly until you get her attention. Gesture with your head in such a way as to communicate that you need her to bring Jerry out into the hallway and probe him about his Grade Two class for the next hour while you keep yourself glued to Ben. She thinks your gesture is aimed at the cannoli. She gives you a nod, wraps a couple up for you, and drops them into her purse with a wink. Might as well gesture for her to wrap up some of the brownies and Nanaimo bars too. You wouldn't want anything to be wasted. On the other guests.

When everything in the room, including your beloved family members, starts to resemble things you might be able to light up and smoke, ask Ben if he wants to join you outside for a quick minute.

"I think I need a bit of air," you say.

"If you want to leave your mother's funeral to smoke, I'm not going to stop you, but I'm not going to enable you either."

"Fine. Just stay here. And by 'here' I mean literally here. This linoleum square. The rest of the floor is lava—I'll be back to save you in two minutes. Two minutes is all I ask."

"But, Care, the potato salad."

"I'm sorry, you know the rules of lava-floor. I'm afraid you're going to have to wait. Two minutes!"

*

The weather, it seems, does not want to enable you either. Fortunately, the church has an awning. Unfortunately, the church has an overzealous usher who takes it upon himself to strictly enforce the "no smoking within five feet of the church door" rule. You've barely pulled out your lighter when he opens the door to chastise you with a simple "nuh-uh" and points to the hand-drawn sign taped to the glass: "Don't make us choke on your second-hand smoke." Apparently the "us" in question is a group of toddler-drawn crayon people with the ability to cry tears the size of their hands.

"There's no one else even out here," you protest. "There's no one to choke even if I wanted to choke someone!"

He taps the sign with his index finger in response.

"You must have us mistaken for Sacred Heart Hotel," he says when you poke your head back in to ask if there's an umbrella you could borrow. "You know, the Lord can give you the strength you need if you only ask him." He rocks his walrus-body back on his heels, gripping the lapels of his jacket for support.

"I dunno, I've been asking for a pony since I was seven, and he's yet to deliver."

"The Lord is not Santa Claus."

"You should let him know the white beard makes it easy to get confused," and you're out the door, six feet into the parking lot, under the protection of nothing.

*

Ben will have to understand why you need to smoke in the car. Just this one time. There must be a dead mother clause in the agreement. And if you've learned anything from the commercials, no smell is immune to a couple sprays of Febreze.

Running across the parking lot, the heel of your ankle boot catches in a pothole, and down you go, gravel imprinting into palms and knees, muddy puddle water splashing into unexpected places like up your nostrils. You feel the hairstyle you gave yourself this morning come loose—mentally you were calling the updo a "chignon," even though you had no idea what a chignon actually looked like or how to fashion one and if pressed to give your hairstyle a more accurate name you would have to call it the "sad mushroom." The heel to your left boot droops from the sole at an odd angle, broken-limb-style.

Silver lining: the rain slides right off the pleather of your skirt and the new holes in your fishnets are barely visible among the other thousand holes in your fishnets.

Limp the rest of the way to your car. Smoke two cigarettes while dripping an imprint of your body onto the upholstery of the driver's seat. If you were the sort of person who believed in life after death, you might watch the rain beading on the windshield and think about your mother, standing atop a bulbous grey cloud, face haloed in heavenly, lemony light. She would tilt her head and sigh one of her classic "I'm not mad, I'm only disappointed in you, but okay, if I'm being perfectly honest I'm also quite mad" sighs.

"See? See? Didn't I tell you?" she would say, clucking her tongue.

"Tell me what? Not to wear fishnet stockings to a funeral? Probably, but you also told me women shouldn't drink beer and tampons are only for trollops so I've had to make some of my own decisions here."

"You better not be buying Kate tampons! No man will want her if she's been deflowered by a tampon!" She would say, visibly shaken, putting her transparent ghost hands onto her transparent ghost hips.

"Well I've let her ride a horse so I think she's already ruined beyond repair," you would say calmly, letting the smoke roll casually out one corner of your mouth.

But since you are not a believer, you only watch the rain beading on the windshield and think about thinking this.

*

Return to the church basement wearing a papier-mâché helmet (a.k.a.: your hair when wet).

"Carrie, what the hell happened to you? Your knees are bleeding!" Tina grabs you by the forearms, the brim of her hat jabbing you in the forehead. "Did some other lady of the evening think you were working her corner?"

"Apparently smoking is a sin," you tell her. "I got... smited? I got... smote?"

"Did you win the wet T-shirt contest at least?" You look down to your barely B-cups, the now-sheer fabric of your black blouse Saran-Wrapped to your breasts. Somehow your chest still barely noticeable. Your go-to description for Tina has always been "just like me, except blonde and busty." Today, for instance, she wears a black cardigan, only the top two buttons of which are undone and yet the effortless meeting of her pillowy breasts is plainly visible—the meeting of your own breasts also occurs effortlessly if you bend at the waist, completely doubling yourself over, and then push them uncomfortably across the vast expanse of your breastbone where they will touch for the briefest of moments before springing apart like the wrong ends of magnets.

A scan of the room and you find Izzy in the same place you left her, but where did Ben go? Was it too much to ask that he remain glued to a one-square-foot tile, face the wall, talk to no one but your emotionally-unstable sister? And if Tina is no longer laughing at dad-level puns or hearing about the infamous Grade Two glue stick heist of '09, does that mean she's shirked her duties or has Jerry finally realized he's overpaid his respects by at least half an hour? Ask Tina casually.

"So, um, I suppose Jerry took off running? More important things to do than comfort an ex-family? A How to Cheat Without Getting Caught convention to go to?"

"Your five o'clock," Tina says.

You whip your head to the left.

"Have you even seen a clock before?"

You whip your head to the right. Ben and Jerry in your five o'clock. In a conversation. A conversation which does not appear, from where you stand with your mouth agape, to be the precursor to any sort of spontaneous duel. By a peculiar twist of fate, you could really go for a pint of Cherry Garcia right now.

- -

Fact: Ben & Jerry's makes 63 flavours of ice cream.

- -

Fact: Eating 63 pints of ice cream will mend a broken heart faster than you can say "Type 2 diabetes," which is hopefully also faster than you can eat 63 pints of ice cream.

- -

Not until this exact moment do you notice the striking similarities between the man to whom you were wed and the man with whom you are living out of wedlock. You notice, for instance, the ease with which they converse with strangers, the way they laugh like dolphins trying to echolocate, even the way they rub their respective, immaculately trimmed beards between their thumbs and index fingers, and their apparent love of powdered-sugar doughnuts. Also: what's up with your thing for teachers? You hated school.

The prodigal daughter chooses this moment to return to your side, watches her ex-step-father and her mother's relatively new live-in boyfriend having a jovial time without the need for either of you to moderate, and says, "Wow, Mom, that's fucked up," at which point you can't argue or even tell her to watch her language because the two of you are, for once, if not exactly on the same page, at least in the same very large library with many distinct sections and many diverse categories of books and other types of media.

If you have begun dating your ex-husband's doppelgänger and not realized it until your mother's funeral, turn to page 886 where you will find a pier. Walk off it.

"Mom, did my dad also have a beard and dress like a train conductor from an old-timey black-and-white movie?"

"Kate, do me a favour. Let's pretend I haven't just swapped versions of the same man for over a decade. It's your grandmother's funeral. We should be thinking of her, not me, okay?"

Before she can answer, two heavy hands land on each of your shoulders. You turn around to find your nose pressed against a fake tuxedo.

"Carrie, how you holding up?" Howie asks, pulling you in for an over-cologned bear hug. You pull away coughing.

"I'm fine, Howie. You really don't have to stay for the wake. Nice enough of you to come to the funeral. Really."

"Oh, my pleasure. Seth asked if anyone would volunteer to go as a work representative and I told him I'd be glad to go because of our—" He lowers his voice. "History," he finishes with a wink.

"YOU TOLD OUR BOSS WE HAVE A HISTORY?!"

Perhaps you should have also lowered your voice.

"Well at least he looks nothing like Ben or Jerry," Kate says.

"Bless us, every one." You make a clumsy sign of the cross—does it go left to right or right to left?—and excuse yourself to the ladies' room.

"I have to go wash my knees," you say to whoever is listening (everyone).

Lean on the Support of Close Friends, Really Lean, That's What They're There For, Just Make Your Body Dead Weight and Let Go (and see if they'll go get you some snacks)

Tina's in town for another day, but tells you in the bathroom where she helps you re-chignon your hair that she can't come over after the wake to cook you brunch.

"And it's like four o'clock. Not really brunch time."

"The grief wants what the grief wants." She contorts your hair with the dexterity of a balloon-animal artist. "Hey, make it into a giraffe and I'll tip you extra."

You watch her reflection in the mirror, hypnotized by the bounce of her bosom.

"Well, the grief will have to wait for its pancakes. I told Mimi and Peppi I'd be over for dinner."

"Visiting your sick, elderly, adorably-nicknamed grand-parents can wait!" you tell her. Stamp your foot and cross your arms, shake your head until your ponytail wriggles free.

"Care, the petulant fake-tantrum bit doesn't really work with the street-walker outfit—I'm getting a lot of mixed signals. And it literally can't wait—they could die at any moment." She wrangles your hair back into her grasp with more force than the first time.

"Well, so could I! I have the diet of an unchaperoned kid at a birthday party! I haven't been to a doctor in years! And I hear most of the experts have finally concluded that smoking is, in fact, bad for your health."

"Care, isolated Amazonian tribes know how bad smoking is for your health," she says, mouth full of bobby pins.

"And one time, after I washed my sheets, I got too lazy to put them back on, so I slept without sheets for a whole week. No pillowcases either. Just the comforter. A whole week. Monday to Monday."

Tina says she has no idea what that has to do with anything.

"And I'm always forgetting to empty the lint trap on the dryer. We're one large load of towels away from an electrical fire over here."

She shuts you up by asking if you want to come visit her grandparents with her.

Suddenly remember all the things you have to do. Netflix won't watch itself.

"Look, we can go grab a drink once they go to bed," she says.

"Perfect, what time do they go to bed? 5:30? Happy hour isn't over until seven. We'll have plenty of time." You leave the bathroom, hair a perfect, coiled snake.

*

In a surge of maternal love, you ask Kate to come with you and Tina. In a surge of psychosis, Kate agrees to come.

"Uh, yeah, sure, fine, An-DREY-uh is working tonight anyways," she says, from the armchair, nose in *The Bell Jar*.

"That's the spirit!"

Ben voices his concerns about taking a sixteen-year-old to a "bar," but you assure him the "restaurant-pub" you're going to leans more heavily towards "restaurant" than "pub."

"They really downplay the pub side of things. Trust me, it's very 'Please Wait to Be Seated, Do You Need a Kid's Menu?' They wait until at least eleven to release the naked go-go dancers."

"Mm-hmm, you're the mom," he says from the sofa, nose in a biography of Robert E. Lee.

*

Unfortunately, the sign on the front door of the restaurant-pub that says "No Minors" indicates you might be mistaken about the nature of the place.

"Great," Kate says, "I suppose you'd like me to just wander the streets for a few hours. Do you have a piece of cardboard and a marker I could use to make myself a sign, or should I just ask passing strangers for their spare change so I can buy myself a hot dog and go eat it under the bridge?"

"Don't be ridiculous. I would obviously give you a toonie for the hot dog."

"We could try another place?" Tina suggests.

"Oh, but I just spent ten minutes parallel-parking right in front of this place," you whine.

"We're downtown, we can just walk somewhere else," Tina says to the restaurant-pub's front window, which she is using as a mirror, as she reapplies her lipstick.

"Walk? You're going to make me walk? After my mother just died? You know it's my least favourite form of transportation after Segway, steamboat, and bicycle built for more than one person."

You make the executive decision that for the night, Kate is eighteen.

But act mature about it and make her pinkie-swear she'll order a Shirley Temple.

Examine her outfit: sneakers, a denim button-up shirt, black pants made to look like jeans but with the elasticity of a gymnastics leotard in case she should feel the need to practice her floor routine.

"Do up all the buttons of your shirt, all the way up to your neck. Yes, even that last one."

"What? Why?" She bats your hands away from her buttons.

"I don't know why! But it seems like the responsible thing to do before you bring your underage daughter into a bar!"

*

When the floppy-haired server, who seems to be wearing suspenders of his own volition, comes over and says, "We're all legal here, right ladies?" say something like, "Aren't you sweet! Thinking I might be seventeen when we're here to celebrate my twenty-fifth birthday." Maybe you'll also score some free cake.

But then Kate will order her Shirley Temple with a shot of Grey Goose because she knows you're paying and that you can't now tell the server you brought a minor into the establishment. You kick her shin under the table.

"Oh, you don't want to add an expensive shot like that to a Shirley Temple! It'll ruin the delicate balance of the orange juice-Sprite-grenadine combination."

"It's true," the server nods. "You'd be better off with a shot of Smirnoff. Won't be able to taste the difference with all the other stuff. And Smirnoff's on special tonight."

How perfect! You can supervise your underage daughter getting tipsy for half-price. You imagine the conversation you'll have with Ben later while mopping Kate's puke from the bathroom walls.

"Kate, honey," Tina says with a hand on your daughter's shoulder, "the doctor said half a glass of wine a week is fine, but vodka... probably not the best idea. We don't want your baby to end up like all the ones your sister had."

"Right, I'm pregnant," Kate says, and then after the server has backed away slowly as if from a wild animal, she begins rubbing her flat sixteen-year-old belly. "I really hope it's a girl so I can name her after you, Mom."

Threaten to ask for a kid's menu and some crayons so she has something else to do with her hands.

*

Naturally, when you and Tina get together the two of you start acting like the incredulous hard-of-hearing:

"What?!"

"No, you didn't!"

"You can't be serious!"

"You said what to your boss?!"

"You told him you had to leave work early to go buy tampons?!"

"You told him you accidentally bought regular absorbency on an extra-heavy day?"

Kate soon tires of this, rudely changes the subject, punishes you for not allowing her a twelve-dollar shot of vodka by turning to Tina and asking about her father.

"So, Tina, were you friends with my dad in high school?" She pops a maraschino into her mouth, nonchalant as if she'd asked about the weather in Florida.

Tina looks to you. Shake your head aggressively but also non-perceptively.

"Um, I don't really remember." Tina grabs her martini glass, concentrates on fishing out an olive.

You miss the days when Kate would punish you by making you play Barbies for ninety minutes, repeatedly insisting you played it wrong, adding another ten minutes per infraction. You really were a great mother from the ages of four until twelve.

"Okay, well what *do* you remember about him? Jock? Science nerd? Band geek? Emo kid? Bro? Brony? Techie? Indie kid? B-Squad? Floater?"

"You guys actually use all those? In our day we had jocks, geeks, and stoners. That's it. A simpler time."

"Okay, so which was he?"

Tina looks around for the server. "Um." Looks at you. "Uh, geek? But with the good looks and charming personality of a jock and the non-violent, kumbaya attitude of a stoner."

"If you just told me his last name, I could Facebook him, just to see what he looks like, maybe ask about his medical history."

"I'm sure I don't remember his last name," Tina says. "All I know is that he never ever did drugs and neither should you."

"Mom, I don't get why you refuse to tell me anything about him. What, is his last name Hitler or Stalin or... Kardashian or something?"

"Because I don't think a Facebook message is the proper way to meet your father." You promise to her all about him when she's ready.

"When I'm *ready*? Every other kid is ready to meet their father when they're like a minute old."

"Well, I just want you to make sure you're mature enough to handle finding out you're a Kardashian."

Kate calls you "impossible." You watch her try to tie the stem of her cherry into a knot inside her mouth.

Tina puts a hand on Kate's forearm. "Hey, what if your mom promised to tell you when you turned eighteen? Full disclosure on your eighteenth birthday, wouldn't that be fair?"

"I gotta pee," Kate says in response, withdraws the untied stem from her mouth and places it on her cocktail napkin. "Don't let them throw this away." You watch her saunter through the crowded restaurant with the confidence of someone much older.

"I don't get it," Tina says, lowering her voice unnecessarily.

"There's nothing to get. I decided to have a baby, he didn't."

"But maybe he would have decided too if you would've given him the option."

"Yes, 'cause that's the dream of every seventeen-year-old boy."

"Okay, so why not tell her now? Is he in jail or something?"

"I have no idea," you tell her and you're not lying. You've been meaning to do some research—you've even entered his name into the Google search bar two or three times, but you've never been able to put finger to the "enter" key.

"I know you don't want to hear this, but I think she has the right to know."

It all sounds so cliché. Kate showing up on his doorstep without calling, his four-year-old son answering the door, thinking she's selling something. It's a scene from a Lifetime TV movie, the kind you would watch, scoffing, only if the remote was out of immediate reach.

"Please, no. You sound just like my mother. If I had let her know anything at all about who knocked me up, she would've told Kate herself."

When Kate returns from the washroom, Tina proposes a toast to your mother.

"This is a wake, I suppose," Tina says. "Do you guys want to say something?"

"To Mom," you start and realize you have no idea how to finish.

"Thanks for always being there," Kate says, Shirley Temple in the air. You cheers her with an empty glass.

Things That Remind You of Your Mother

1. Internet pop-ups.

2. Pancakes that look fully cooked, but upon the first bite reveal their gooey, uncooked centres, which you ravenously consume anyway because they are still, by definition, pancakes.

3. Children dressed up on Hallowe'en as mummies, costumes you know are homemade from toilet paper and cloths that used to be white but, upon inheriting a greyish tinge, were confined to the "rag bin." When it starts to snow (because October in Alberta), their costumes begin to wilt and droop and you can see the black turtlenecks they're wearing underneath, making them look like your newspaper that is always soggy even though it rarely ever rains in Calgary and thus causes you to be awfully suspicious of what your mail carrier does with these newspapers before delivery.

4. The free gifts with purchase from the Estée Lauder counter at The Bay. (i.e., your birthday gifts from the ages of 12-25).

5. Internet pop-ups that warn you about internet pop-ups.

- -

You remember coming home to Airdrie from school in Edmonton—far enough away to necessitate living in residence on campus but close enough that you promised your mother you'd be home every weekend to help with Kate. When you did come home—not every weekend because a crying baby in the next room did not make studying and writing term papers any easier—you would spend the day marveling over Kate, holding her gingerly, fearfully, as if she were someone else's baby.

"What precious tiny fingers, what big beautiful eyes," you would say as if her real mother were standing with you in the room and you were offering her a compliment. You would volunteer to change Kate's soiled diapers as though you were doing her real mother a favour, and when she cried you would look to your mother expectantly, eager to hand her off.

"I just don't know her moods right now," you'd say, non-apologetically.

After putting Kate to bed, you would call Tina and the two of you would drive the half hour to Calgary, meet up with friends who had since migrated to the city, spend the evening drinking at a hotel bar you couldn't afford, hoping to meet rich oil executives or investment bankers who might pick up the tab. More often than not, you would stay the night on a city friend's couch, returning to Airdrie sometime the next afternoon, hungover and sluggish.

Your mother would sigh and cluck her tongue and hand you a bottle she'd already warmed in the microwave, tested on her inner wrist.

- -

People With Whom You Share Cubicle Walls

1. *Howie*
Age: Middle-aged.
Age he pretends to be in chatrooms: 28
Martial status: Single. So single.
Have you dated? Explain: Yes. Only once right after you split from Jerry and were feeling particularly unlovable. He took you to an Applebee's, where he proceeded to get tanked off frozen strawberry daiquiris and then asked the server for separate bills. You had to drive him "home," which is how you discovered he lives on a friend's couch and keeps his clothes in a duffel bag. Needless to say, you married him a month later. (You didn't.)

Most annoying workplace habit: Playing air guitar along with the depressing adult contemporary radio station which promises "light rock, less talk" and is all your company considers "workplace-appropriate music." On a side note, your company policies have started to remind you more and more of your mother, who had been convinced that listening to rock 'n' roll "made a girl want to take off her blouse."

Manner of dress: Faded, ripped jeans, too-tight Rolling Stones T-shirts, and a bandana tied around left forearm, serving no apparent purpose.

Productivity level: -4

2. Bethany Marie

Age: 36

Age she acts: 50

Martial status: Destined for crazy cat lady-ness.

Number of cats in current possession: Four; five until last week when Pickles was gunned down by a pickup truck (i.e., committed suicide) after wandering (i.e., escaping) through a hole in the side gate.

Have you offered Poncho to replace Pickles? Yes, but she refused to take your inheritance and insists you need Poncho to help with the grieving process.

Manner of dress: Floral muumuus.

Did you just type "muumuus" because you liked how many U's it has? Guilty.

Most annoying workplace habit: Logging onto animal websites to audibly coo over kittens in teacups and puppies snuggling with bunnies and whatever chipmunks do that makes them so goddamn adorable. Then forwarding the pictures to you and expecting a response other than "I really hope fur coats make a comeback this year." *Productivity level:* 72%

3. *Ian*

Age: Fifty-five-ish.

Age he acts: Fifty-five-ish.

Marital Status: Possibly dating a younger, mysterious man named Marcus who pops by the office a few times a month to take Ian to lunch. Ian has neither confirmed nor denied your suspicions, despite your probing questions of "So this Marcus?" and "You two seem close?"

Are you friends? You wouldn't say friends, but you appreciate the way Ian berates Howie's attempts at youth and hipness, and the biweekly speeches he gives to Bethany about why she needs to "get laid" or at least start dressing "sluttier."

Most annoying workplace habits: Speaking as if every third word happened to be cosmically italicized and using patronizing finger quotes, often employing both tics simultaneously.

Manner of Dress: Sweaters, chinos, and vests from the Gap, neon striped sneakers and pinky rings from trips to various foreign countries.

Productivity level: Five out of five stars.

- -

Making profiles of your coworkers is so much more satisfying than inputting random numbers into arbitrary spreadsheet boxes so you decide to make a profile for yourself:

- -

4. *Carrie*

Age: 29

Excuse Me? 30

Try Again: It is extremely impolite to ask a lady her age, weight, or when she last washed her hair.

Marital status: Divorced from Jerry, shacking up with Ben, no plans for remarriage.

Dependents: Kate, daughter, age 16; Poncho, reluctantly adopted cat, age unknown, presumably very old considering you barely remember a time pre-Poncho.

Interesting facts: Refuses to eat at Applebee's; still can't figure out how to work the iPad her boyfriend got her for Christmas; has trouble explaining to people (including herself) exactly what she does for a living.

Annoying workplace habits: Gets obsessive-compulsive over FreeCell games; finds feeding the shredder therapeutic; answers all serious questions with sarcasm.

Manner of dress: Currently in mourning attire: black jeans, black turtleneck, black boots. Was going for "Audrey Hepburn chic" but has begun to question whether she is pulling it off after daughter (see above) asked if she was performing slam poetry later.

FreeCell Stats: 84% to win.

- -

Game Over.
Sorry, you lose.
There are no more legal moves.
Do you want to play again?
Y/N?

Making a Triumphant Return to the "Real World" (a.k.a. the place where your bed isn't)

When you return to work after your allotted two-day grieving period, you find that Seth, your boss, has instituted a "no-jeans policy" to create a "more professional working environment, which will surely increase the morale and the productivity of the staff." You decide you need more clarification on the recent prohibition of denim so you e-mail Seth asking him to clarify what exactly constitutes "appropriate" work attire.

*Carrie sent on 03 11 9:28am: <<Will dress pants suffice or should I be looking into renting a three-piece tuxedo for five-day intervals?>> *Flagged as Urgent**

Seth sent on 03 11 3:12pm: <<Carrie, the new dress code is clear in its mandate: no jeans. Anything else is acceptable attire.>>

Naturally, your mind will start to wander to all "acceptable" forms of legwear. Start with sweatpants, move to Spandex leggings in shocking fuchsia, end up somewhere down the progression with lederhosen, though you're not entirely sure what lederhosen look like exactly, whether they can take the place of pants altogether, or if some other apparatus is required in conjunction with them. At any rate, your closet does not overflow with German apparel but you do own a fair number of sweatpants, many of which are a few sizes too large and feature a handsome spectrum of stains from bleach to coffee. You settle on a particularly homely pair of black ones (you are still in mourning, after all) with a satisfying number of holes and a stain of unknown origin but with the peculiar property of being neon green. They also feature those handsome little elastic bands which bunch at the ankles, making you look like a helium balloon character from the Macy's Thanksgiving Day parade. The drawstring whose job description consists only of holding up the waist has since departed, but you do not let this stop you. Ian has left his cubicle to meet with an advertising client and has changed out of his athletic high-tops (note the lack of policy regarding casual footwear) into the dress shoes he keeps in the bottom drawer of his filing cabinet. You swipe one of the neon yellow shoelaces from his unattended Nikes and repurpose it as your new belt. Should you choose to go for a nighttime jog you will be both comfortable *and* reflective.

Choose to go for a nighttime jog: turn to the last page of this book and then close the book because you have clearly chosen the wrong book. Choose another book: **Why I Am Better Than Everyone Else** *or* **How I Found a Horse This High and Managed to Get Up Here.**

Choose to go for a nighttime walk to the gelato shop two blocks from your house: keep reading, this book is for you.

Wear sweatpants every day since receiving the anti-denim memo. Try to get your coworkers on board.

"You can't support this fabric fascism!" you tell them, but they don't want to get in trouble for signing your petition, "Down with Fabricism ."

More specifically, wear the same pair of sweatpants in succession without washing them. You no longer mind when Poncho scratches at your pant legs for more wet cat food after his third helping. You encourage him.

"Scratch your heart out, Poncho!" you say, at which point he predictably stops scratching. You wonder if you were to encourage Poncho to scratch your brand-new tweed bag as well, would he stop scratching your brand new tweed bag? But you figure him much too wily for reverse psychology.

Your boss will soon take notice of how you have basically become Gandhi, at which point he will have no choice but to retreat, dejected, into his office and retract his previous statute, replacing it with a "no-sweatpants policy" with which you will happily comply while wearing your beautifully worn-in denim. After a week, however, the only people who seem to take any notice are Ian (because that was apparently his lucky shoelace) and Ben (because you haven't been bothering to change out of your sweats when you come home to ensure that they achieve maximum contact with all stain-inducing cleaning products, food items, and the now-constant cat fur in your home). After three more workdays, Ben all but gives you an ultimatum.

"Seriously, Carrie, I feel like I'm dating a homeless person. And those have to be Jerry's pants. I don't appreciate the daily reminder of your ex-husband."

Don't confirm that they once belonged to Jerry, because that would make you the cold-hearted woman who flaunts her ex-marriage in her current boyfriend's face, nor deny it, because you wouldn't want Ben to think pants that could fit a grown man actually belong to you. You know that Jerry would have found the humour in your sweatpants protest, even if they employed your ex-husband's sweatpants, but nevertheless, head out to buy work-appropriate "trousers." Keep your distance from anything labelled "slacks." For your own safety.

- -

Conversation with shop girl:

SG: Hi there, ma'am, is there anything I can help you find today?
You: Ma'am? I'm only thirty-four.
SG: I wouldn't have guessed so old! You look great for your age!
You: Oh, aren't you sweet. I need some pants. For work. Black.
SG: I have some beautiful peg pants in organic cotton!
You: I'll level with you: I don't pay extra for organic produce and I don't rub fruits and vegetables on my skin, I eat them. Also, I'm not sure what "peg pants" are but I imagine they're pants shaped like pegs, and that's all tickety-boo, but aren't all pants peg-shaped? What other shapes do pants come in? I mean, okay, you've got your bell-bottoms and Hammer pants and—

SG: Tickety-boo?

You: It's a thing we said in the '30s. Don't worry about it.

- -

Buy a pair of organic cotton and Spandex blend pants. The Spandex will allow you to sit comfortably with your feet up on your desk. The organic cotton will make you feel good about yourself, despite their resemblance to your mother's entire hospital wardrobe. Wash them using non-organic laundry detergent before wearing them so you don't feel too good about yourself. No one likes a show-off. Buy a button-up blouse if your other blouses are missing buttons and you're too lazy to sew them back on. Do not allow Shopgirl to talk you into buying a patterned scarf to tie around your neck. You do not work as a flight attendant, nor do you often find yourself complaining about having a cold neck.

You tried to get Kate to go shopping with you but she said, "Please, Mother, I'd rather watch you watch a documentary about mulch," before returning to her new hobby: turning her "emotional energy" into abstract paintings using only black and grey. Poncho licked his nether regions in a way that translated to the same thing, except Poncho would never call you "Mother" and Poncho turns his "emotional energy" into black and grey abstract art in the litter box.

*

You remember when work used to be fun. Bridget, your boss before Seth, rarely came out of her office (i.e., rarely took a break from filling her nostrils with illegal narcotics) to tell you and your cubicle-mates to quit your games of Eraser Hockey. You fondly remember the time you borrowed her stationery and issued a memo to Howie declaring the following Friday to be "Hawaiian

Shirt Day," or maybe your exact words were "Mandatory Wear Your Hawaiian Shirt to Work or You Will be Fired Day." That Friday Howie met with the company's regional manager for a performance review. When he later woke Bridget up from a nap on the bathroom floor to ask why no one else had participated in Mandatory Hawaiian Shirt Day, she mistook him for a waiter at Bahama Breeze and ordered a frozen daiquiri. She really was your favourite boss.

Interestingly, the reason for Bridget's eventual termination was completely unrelated to her drug use. Unless she sold the stolen office supplies in order to buy more drugs. Or didn't show up that one week because she was on a bender. Or only sexually harassed the interns because she was high.

Seth, who has the sex appeal of a sexless shrew-mole, who never once played Eraser Hockey, found himself promptly promoted.

- -

Actual, verifiable fact: A group of moles is called a "labour."

- -

Things You Can Accomplish While Driving to Work

1. Shaving your legs if you a have one cup of water (no lid) and one of those new razors with the shaving cream attached to it in a handy, solid bar (and not having to wear opaque nylons as part of your "workplace-appropriate attire")

2. Reading at least four pages of the eight-page report from work which Seth emailed to you yesterday at 3:59

with a note shouting "Important! Must be read by start of day tomorrow!"

3. Going over in your mind exactly what you will say, in a ten-point speech, when you confront Seth about why you should receive a raise of at least five percent. (Point 1: Because four percent would not be enough.)

4. Making up important lists for yourself and writing them down with your eyeliner pencil on the back of fast-food napkins you found stuffed in your glove box. (E.g.: "Things You Can Get Accomplished While Driving to Work.")

5. Applying said eyeliner if you no longer wish to have vision in your left eye.

- -

Fact: People shaving their legs at traffic lights cause 0.003% of car accidents.

- -

Fact: People trying to merge while applying eye liner cause 0.07% of car accidents.

- -

Fact: That truck didn't signal and had already braked before you entered the intersection.

- -

Seth tells you half an hour into your shift on Wednesday that he must "let you go." As reason for your dismissal he cites your numerous late arrivals. Furthermore, he wants you to know that your protesting the dress code by wearing your oldest sweatpants for a week straight did not go unnoticed (you: 1, inane work policies: 0). In addition, he does not think you contribute to the workplace morale and that "it is plain to see" you just do not value your job. You argue the contrary.

Tell him you absolutely, one-hundred-percent love your job. Seth will then hand you the rough draft to an article you've been using company time to work on and apparently left in the break room titled, "Reasons Why I Hate My Job."

"But my work ethic is second to none!"

"Yes, if I ranked the work ethic of everyone in the office, you would be second from the bottom and the only one below you is George's five-year-old son who he brings here when preschool has a day off and he can't find a sitter—and even then his drawings of zoo animals really do brighten up the place and lift spirits around here."

You ask why he couldn't have fired you yesterday before you left work, because then you wouldn't have had to wake up early this morning, put on your newly enforced "workplace-appropriate attire" (does he plan to reimburse you for that, by the way?) and drive across the city, wasting your gas, contributing to ozone depletion with your exhaust fumes, putting the lives of innocent pedestrians in peril as you "diligently read over, for the second time, all eight pages of the extremely important and useful report."

Be sure to ask whether he just decided to fire you that morning. Was he on his way to work, sitting on the heated seat in his company car, sipping a tall non-fat double-whipped mocha-latte when he decided he could easily do without one sloppily-dressed employee? If so, suggest he go home, perhaps right now, and sleep on it.

"No sense making a hasty decision," tell him.

He tells you that, no, he did not just decide to "let you go" this morning while he was sipping his tall non-fat double-whipped mocha-latte, which he actually repeats verbatim, making you wonder if you are the prophet of hot beverages and how you might make a profit from such a talent.

As it turns out, Seth did "sleep on it." He decided to fire you yesterday after you "sauntered, unapologetically, into work forty-five minutes late," but then he thought to his "kind-hearted self" that he should give you the day to redeem yourself. Plus, yesterday was the one-week anniversary of your mother's death and he is "not that cruel." But when you ducked out of work twenty minutes early, he decided that the "let go" would be final, though of course you were five floors down the elevator shaft by then. Seth thought about calling you that evening but knows from experience that these things go over better in person. Usually. He'll tell you some anecdote about a "cubicle person" he once fired over the phone who cried and pleaded until he hung up, only to then turn around and show up at work the next day, bright-eyed and seemingly unaware that she was prohibited from so much as touching a company pen, so he had to fire said person a second time, you see? The only anecdote you'll be in the mood for at the moment is the one where the oppressed employee overthrows the oppressive boss with a staple gun.

"Seth, I'd like to remind you that my mother just died. This is a very difficult time for me." You say this so coldly not even you believe it's a valid excuse for anything. "I would think this company would be a little more supportive," you add.

He reminds you that you did receive a two-day grieving period.

"But aren't you always saying that we're a family here? Shouldn't I get more than the equivalent of a weekend—"

"Didn't you get the sympathy card we sent? I had everyone in the office sign it."

"Well yes, but—"

"And Howie was at the funeral? He better not have used your funeral as an excuse to get out of work and go paintballing—"

"Yes, he was at my *mother's* funeral," you correct him.

"Your workplace behaviour has been an issue since long before you found out your mother was dying. Which was some time ago now." Up until this point you have heard only yourself speak of your mother's death like it was just the inevitable thing that it was. Like a vacation you planned months ago but somehow forgot to pack for. However, such a matter-of-fact tone used by someone other than yourself leaves you with an empty, hollow feeling in your gut that you can't quite place.

You have no choice now but to retreat to your cubicle with the almost-empty cardboard box that Seth handed you (he threw in the rough draft of your most promising article as a parting gift, though that seems a little like re-gifting now that you think about it) and begin packing your things, and some things which do not technically belong to you, such as the company staple gun. Unfortunately, packing up the company shredder seems a little too conspicuous. Throw Kate's baby pictures in the box with all the unorganized loose leaf paper scattered on your desk, under your desk, in your drawers, on top of your computer, with grand, sweeping gestures. The spreadsheets, charts, and graphs mean nothing to you, but continue to shovel this stuff into your box with great fervour.

Occasionally, make a point of stopping packing your box as if you've become too drained of breath to continue. Put a hand to your forehead and make sure to sigh audibly. Your neighbours predictably peek their nosy noses over the tops of their cubicles. You'll want to put on a good show for them, so start muttering things under your breath such as "Oh, what is a poor, unemployed mother to do?" and "Who will feed my daughter now?" Ian asks if you've been "let go" in a whisper audible within a twenty-cubicle foot radius. Naturally, he uses finger quotes as he says "let go." Stop packing, ask him what he thinks.

"I think this is positively unconscionable, is what I think. Making you come into work just to let you go. Should've have called you and let you stay in pajamas all day, poor thing."

Begin packing again, this time swiping Bethany's cat-shaped tape dispenser.

- -

Reasons You Should Not Have Been "Let Go"

1. Your mother just died.

2. You're a recent divorcée.

3. You have a little girl at home who needs to be fed, clothed, and sheltered, and the only one else here with mouths to feed is Bethany, but too bad for you Kate won't eat cat food. Or normal people food like Hamburger

Helper or Rice-a-Roni, instead insisting on elitist "super-foods" like arugula and sunflower butter.

4. You're the only one in the office who knows that "fricative" is not a euphemism for a swearword.

5. Cancer is hereditary.

6. Indeterminate organs of yours have started to feel sore. You'd venture to say "precancerous." Pre-Herbie, even.

- -

Leave the list on your now-tidy desk (the first time you've seen your desk in such a state since your very first work week), give the office one dramatic sweep of your eyes, one highly emphatic sigh, and bust through the doors before Seth can have the satisfaction of calling security. Howie will follow you out, bear-hugging you from behind. He promises that "this will not be the end," prompting you to make a mental promise to block his work number, cell number, and email address as soon as you get home.

Dear _____,

So you are replacing me. Apparently you are great with numbers, enjoy mind-numbing work, and will never need to come in late or need to leave early. Kudos to you. How often do you have to oil your joints and update your computer chip? Does it hurt when you have a power surge?

I purposefully broke the lever on the side of the chair before I left so you couldn't adjust it. Welcome to a life of back pain. Check the drawers—that's right, I stole everything. Here's hoping Staples has a sale soon.

I took the liberty of telling everyone at the office some things about you:

1. You love to donate to worthy causes, buy things other people's children are selling, and help fund school trips.

2. You have severe allergies to sugar and being offered baked goods offends you.

3. You need to pay back the money you squandered on a decade-long methamphetamine addiction, so you are more than willing to work overtime for anyone who needs to leave early.

4. You are single and looking for a conservative woman who shares your number-one interest: cats.

5. You are single and looking for a liberal man who shares your number-one interest: air guitar.

Not only does your job consist of entering sales data into the weekly spreadsheets, but it's also your duty to write articles for the company newsletter. Do not start on the spreadsheets until you finish writing the newsletter— the most important aspect of your job. In fact, Seth has informed me that his first task for you is to finish the article I started entitled, "Reasons Why I Hate My Job." It's a little tongue-in-cheek piece. Very funny. Sure to boost everyone's spirits around here. You will find the first draft in the top right drawer. Bring it to him by the end of the day for bonus points.

Signed,
Your friend, Carrie

*

Tell the two people who love and admire you most, that you, their personal hero have lost your job. Turn to page 43 to crush their gentle spirits and make them question everything they thought to be true and good in this world.

Flip to page 56 to avoid informing Ben and Kate that you, the employee of the year, have joined the ranks of the unemployed. Continue to get ready for work in the morning, preparing a "workplace-appropriate" outfit that does not include sweat-pants or jeans.

*

On the second day of your newfound freedom, you get into a heated argument with Ben for taking too long in the shower, thus, making you hypothetically late.

"I could get fired!" you yell at him across the shower curtain, as you flush the toilet. He asks if you've started your period. You hurl a can of shaving cream into the curtain and hope it hits a rib.

You pass Poncho on the way down the stairs. He has plopped himself halfway either up or down and has given up on continuing in either direction. Tell him quitting is not an option as you prod him with your toe. When he finally makes it to the bottom, hold the front door open and tell him to run free. He looks up at you with his stupid, squashy moon-face, but doesn't move. Doesn't even seem curious about what's on the other side of the door.

Clearly you shouldn't have used the word "run."

You find Kate in the kitchen with a bowl of cereal, the boring kind without marshmallows or chocolate flakes or frosted anything or fun activities on the box. Bowl sitting of the counter, she eats standing up.

"How dare we put the kitchen table so far away from the fridge so that you might actually have to walk twelve steps after you get your food. Take a stand, sister! I'm with you!"

She doesn't roll her eyes or groan or tell you to shut up. Actually she says, "Good morning," which means she heard your fight with Ben. Sure, Kate likes Ben well enough (because Ben is as inoffensive as water or bread or Switzerland), but still, like a teeter-totter of emotions, you can count on her to light up whenever you're in a bad mood. Just like your mother, Kate seems to feed off your misery, plug into your negative energy to recharge her batteries. Maybe she will turn this scene into an abstract, grey-scale painting you can hang in the living room above the pile of bricks you bought on sale at Canadian Tire and have configured into a square-shape that you hope will one day take the hint and transform itself into the electric fireplace you know it has the potential to become.

You hand Kate a lunchbag that you're not completely sure has anything in it; it feels suspiciously light. You were so exhausted the night before you didn't even have the energy to change the channel when the eleven o'clock news came on, and your subsequent dreams were much too well-informed for your liking. Hand her a ten-dollar bill just in case. Isn't she too old for you to be making her lunch anyway? You thought she would remove you from lunchbag duty the day you mistook a beer can for a pop can and sent her to school with a Bud Light. As per your inquiry, she assured you that no, other kids' parents surely have not made such a mistake.

*

Instead of driving to work, you drive to a Starbucks-like coffeehouse (in addition to serving overpriced drinks, this coffeehouse serves overpriced drinks you can get spiked with alcohol at an even more overly overprice, anytime after 11 a.m.), located off the ramp you usually take when exiting Deerfoot Trail for work—which, despite its name, is not a dirt trail curving through a picturesque forest full of prancing deer but an eight-lane freeway full of maniacal, pick-up-truck-driving, solipsistic speed-racers—and took today out of habit. You hope you don't run into any ex-coworkers, but are reasonably sure that ten dollars a coffee is out of their price range: when you had gainful employment you would have flat-out refused to pay more than four bucks for a caffeine boost, but curiously, now that your income has become nonexistent, you find yourself able to spend money guilt-free.

Order a drink that costs more than the shoes you're wearing (though in Joe Mama's defense, you did get them in the clearance bin at Old Navy) and take residence in a corner couch with the Classifieds section of the newspaper. At eleven on the dot, order lunch (i.e., a danish) and an Irish coffee, telling the pimply-faced barista not to "skimp" as you lean over the counter watching your milk being frothed into foam. He adds extra whipped cream thinking that's what you don't want "skimped." By noon you have circled a total of no job positions.

Possible Careers

1. Librarian. You enjoy reading and telling other people to be quiet. You also like that calm, musty smell of used books. However, you're not the most organized person in the world, which was made clear to you when you won your ex-office's "Most Disorganized Person Award," though the cataloguing system of putting things wherever you please seems to be working out nicely for your own bookshelf. Mind you, your own bookshelf is full of old Nancy Drews that your mother thought Kate would enjoy reading as much as you did (correct for once—Kate has not read a single mystery).

Other Awards You Won at Your Ex-Office:
a) Least Punctual
b) Most Tardy

2. Coffee Shop Owner. Your first order of business would be to do away with those annoyingly teeny tiny shot-glass thingies that the Baileys gets measured in before it makes its way to the cup. You see no reason why you couldn't just pour it yourself like you are expected to do with the milk and cream.

3. *Teacher.* Surely, the teaching degree is just a formality. Plus, you've now dated two teachers and paid attention to some of the things they told you about their jobs. Plus, you'd already have summers off so you wouldn't have to quit your job every June and look for a new one every September.

4. *Stay-at-home trophy wife.* Though Tina prefers "homemaker" to "trophy wife" and is really tired of you asking her how many homes she's made this week every time you have a phone conversation. If only you could also meet the owner of a chain of retirement homes in the Floridian panhandle.

- -

Just before one o'clock your cell phone rings. Izzy. She consoles you on losing your job. If it was anyone but your sister, you'd be shocked to find out that they knew something you told no one but Tina. But you are not shocked. Izzy claims to work for a pharmaceutical company but of this you have seen no substantial evidence (she has refused to give you free drug samples on at least one hundred occasions). She is more than likely employed by whatever the polite, non-threatening Canadian version of the CIA is.

"It's fine, really. Just don't go putting out a family newsletter, okay?" you tell her.

"I only made a newsletter that one time. But if you need help finding something let me know. I know some people in the hiring departments of some great companies."

You venture to guess that your idea of great and Izzy's idea of great are not one and the same. Unless hers also involves a drink cart that pulls up to your desk every hour on the hour.

"Thanks, Iz. You think you could do me a favour?"

"Name it."

"Since I'm not working at the moment, money's going to be a little hard to come by..."

"Of course, of course. You need a loan." You can almost hear Izzy rustling in her purse for her chequebook.

"Not exactly... More so wondering if you could take Poncho off my hands. You know, like, adopt him? I mean, I've got to buy his food, pay for his vet bill—"

The line goes dead, a final "Pon—" dangling on your lips.

*

Later that week you decide you may have to take your sister up on her offer; you don't know how many more days you can spend slumped in the corner couch of a coffee shop. The staff know you by name, though you don't remember introducing yourself. Yes, you may just have to take Izzy up on her offer—not to find you a job, of course, but to loan you coffee money.

People You're Sure Your Mother Hired From Beyond the Grave to Drive You Insane

1. Every single employee at the coffee shop you should have stopped frequenting when they refused to let you have your mail forwarded there.

2. Poncho. Though likely your mother began his indoctrination years ago.

3. Your daughter's best friend Andrea, whom you still must refer to as "An-DREY-uh," even though you've heard her own mother call her "And-REE-ah," and despite the fact that she has decided to call you by your first name and helps herself to your cans of Diet Mountain Dew, which you later find half-full on your daughter's bedroom floor, making you resort to hiding them in your pantry and drinking them with ice cubes, which results in soda more watery than fizzy.

4. The woman who is at the gym no matter what one day of the month you choose to go and always changes the one working television to the Food Network so you have to watch the preparation of gourmet chocolate-filled croissants as you simulate cross-country skiing and have no way of actually procuring any chocolate-filled croissants, which must be one of the torture methods currently in use in the fight against terrorism.

5. Miss Food Network never ties back her long blonde hair and never breaks a sweat while next to her you drip like a woolly mammoth in the Amazon.

6. Miss Food Network sits her cell phone in the tray on one of two working elliptical trainers and doesn't notice when it rings (loudly) because she has her headphones on, busy learning how to bake a croissant until it's golden like her skin in the wintertime.

- -

Fact: Doctors commonly analyze desired ringtones to determine a person's level of sociopathy.

- -

Fact: You can plead insanity to first-degree murder if your ringtone is the theme song to any sitcom from the early '90s.

- -

Things to Do

—cut down on how much you tip the asshole baristas, which shouldn't be hard since the only time you tipped them more than fifty cents you forgot to take your change
—insist that Kate spend more time at An-DREY-uh's (i.e., suggest she take some juice boxes from the fridge without asking, poke the straws through the tinfoil openings and leave them under a bed in the guestroom)
—buy chocolate croissants, eat them in furious succession, watch stomach turn into a crescent roll
—bake skin until golden brown
—change ringtone from silent to vibrate, leave phone in the tray of elliptical trainer with a handful of nickels, arrange for Tina to call

- -

Three weeks after the funeral, you see Jerry at the gym you both still belong to. After the divorce you thought about making and giving him a schedule of "your" time at the gym and "his" gym time, but the thought of operating on a schedule brought on a two-day wave of nausea. Also, considering you subscribe to a once-a-month fitness regimen, running into your ex hasn't really been an issue for the past five years.

Today, however, you decide once-a-month just might not be enough to counterbalance the whipped cream you've been consuming daily as if it were your job (a part of you has started believing it actually is your job and you're doing great!). Today is also the day Jerry chooses the exact same hour to spend at your mutual gym. On the other side of the room, he and Miss Food Network straddle side-by-side stationary bicycles.

Dismiss this as a coincidence. You even count this as your lucky day because you can actually choose, without interruption, which television channel to watch, also uninterrupted, for the next forty minutes. *Real Housewives of Kenora*, here you come!

But then you see her head turn his way. You catch an exchange of wide smiles and wonder what aspect of being at a gym would ever induce feelings of mutual happiness. You eye her fetching purple outfit with its light blue racing stripes running down the sides of her long legs. A sliver of stomach showing. As you expected, a pancake golden brown. You look down at your skin, white and bumpy like the uncooked batter left over in the bottom of the Tupperware bowl. You regret your baggy T-shirt, a relic of one of Kate's old softball teams. Who the yellow sweat-stains under the arms belong to is anyone's guess.

You invent dialogue anytime you see one of their mouths moving.

"I have a moronic idea! Let's pretend we're bicycling through the south of France!"

"How romantique!"

"I told my ex-wife I would take her to France one day, but I decided to spend all my money on a high-end sport utility vehicle because I didn't care enough about her or the planet."

They dismount their stationary bicycles in unison.

"I'll see you in five minutes when I get out of the locker room—make that ten; I usually need an extra five to stare at myself flexing in the mirror."

"I'll miss you."

"I'll miss you more."

You wish the gym permitted smoking.

Miss Food Network ducks into the women's locker room while Jerry heads for the drinking fountain, located within spitting distance of your machine. Resist the urge to cross the divide with your saliva. Instead, pick up the pace on the elliptical and fake your focus on the television program playing above your head. Maybe he won't see you if you don't make any sudden movements. Don't look at him, don't look at him, don't look at him—yes, you know he's not a dinosaur from *Jurassic Park*, but it still could work. Look down at the machine, push some random buttons until some random lights come on. Hills? No, no, you don't want to fake-ski up a hill. What does this machine think you are, a mountain goat? Where's the button for flat? Flat as a golden pancake. Flat is good, flat is nice. Back to the TV, concentrate—how long have you been watching the Food Network? how did that happen?—look interested, maybe he won't want to distract you from—a commercial break.

"Hi, Carrie."

"Oh, hey there, *you*. Fancy meeting *you* here!" Why are you being weird? Stop being weird. You increase your pace again in an attempt to prove yourself just as fit as Miss Food Network.

"I haven't seen you here lately." Jerry grabs the handle bar of your elliptical trainer for stability and begins stretching his hamstrings. He and your armpits now in dangerously close quarters. You wonder how bad you smell on a scale of one to blue cheese.

"That's weird, cause I'm here *all* the time. Our schedules must conflict." You have trouble getting the sentences out between gasps for oxygen, but increase your pace again nonetheless. You catch Jerry stealing a glance at the display screen on your elliptical: seven minutes and forty-three, forty-four, forty-five seconds.

"Oh are you not working nine-to-five anymore?" Jerry has apparently appointed himself Gym Police. Eight minutes and three, four, five seconds.

"No—I'm still nine-to-five—which is why I usually work out when the gym's really quiet—like three a.m." You have to break every few words or you may stop breathing altogether. Jerry shows no signs of leaving.

"Well, good for you. You look great." Rather than stare at the ceiling, he actually holds eye contact while he says this—his lying has really gotten so much better. He used to lie to your mother all the time. Yes, he loved the sweater she got him for his birthday. No, he doesn't think the snowflake pattern around the collar is "too much." Yes, he wore it just last week, in fact, and can't wait until the next snowfall to wear it again.

"Gotta stay healthy!" you say and follow it up with a fit of smoker's cough to prove your point. Eight minutes and thirty-eight, thirty-nine, forty seconds. Someone has lit the backs of your thighs on fire. Instead of leaving, Jerry begins doing some sort of lunge routine and you wonder why his kneecaps aren't making the loud popping noises that yours do.

"Say hi to Kate for me and tell Ben I'm going to take him up on his offer."

"His offer?" Perhaps you misheard, this level of strenuous exercise now making you delirious.

"Yeah, he asked me to be the fourth on his golf team this spring. Unless you have a problem with—"

"Of course not!" Why would you have a problem with your ex-husband out on the green with your current boyfriend? Why might you find it strange for them to wear matching pastel golf shirts and visors, share a golf cart and a high-five, look into each other's eyes and for a moment feel as though they were looking into a past or future version of themselves?

"I'm happy for you. Ben seems like a great guy."

"The best!"

Miss Food Network waves Jerry over to the juice bar.

"Time to go do some bicycle crunches!"

"You go crunch those bikes! Serves those bike owners right for riding their bikes to the gym!"

"Take care, Care." He gives you the same look of pity he did when he slammed the church door in your face. That door was definitely a metaphor and you wish you had been the one slamming it.

- -

What You Want to Say to Jerry But Can't Because You've Prioritized Breathing Over Speaking

1. Can't you see that I do take care of myself? I am at the gym, aren't I?

2. Okay, I admit I haven't given up smoking, but you clearly haven't given up wearing tank-tops.

3. I look great you say? My pit-stained softball tee is a real crowd-pleaser!

4. Sure, Miss Racing Stripes runs on the treadmill like a goddamn gazelle but look how fast I awkwardly simulate cross-country skiing!

5. Don't feel sorry for me! I am not a charity case! But if you would like to donate, I won't stop you.

- -

Fact: Gazelles consistently win nature's hot body contests.

- -

Swear off the gym for life and stop by the front counter to cancel your membership, turn to page 45.

Hit up the nearest tanning salon and stop wearing "hand-me-ups" from your daughter, flip to page 67.

- -

Carrie's Pros and Cons of Indoor Tanning

Pro: You will achieve that "healthy-looking, bronzed glow" (according to sign on window of accredited tanning salon, Sun Spot, in the basement of your gym).

Con: "People who frequently expose themselves to UV rays are 75% more likely to develop melanoma, the most deadly form of skin cancer, at some point in their lives" (according to accredited medical magazine in the magazine rack next to the stationary bikes on the main level of your gym).

Pro: Indoor tanning provides you with essential vitamin D (according to flyer on counter of accredited tanning salon, Sun Spot).

Con: "Two of the greatest causes of wrinkles are smoking and UV exposure" (according to page 2 of accredited medical magazine).

Pro: Indoor tanning has proven much safer than outdoor tanning (according to fifteen-year-old girl behind desk of accredited tanning salon, Sun Spot).

Con: The lid of the tanning bed could lock in the "down" position, while the wiring malfunctions causing the bed to remain running, frying and bubbling your skin like bacon, while the fifteen-year-old attendant tries to open the door, which you obviously locked and triple-checked because you didn't want anyone to "accidentally" wander into your room and see you lying there naked, but now the firefighters have to come and axe down the door and will see you lying there naked anyway (while you haven't yet completed your weekly regimen of two to three sessions of approximately eight to fifteen minutes in length and still look paler than the ghost of an anemic vegan hippie (according to common sense).

Pro: ...

Con: Death. And even after numerous skin grafts you will have a closed-casket funeral (your eyes definitely also closed).

Con: Ben can never find love again, becomes a hoarder, dies in a freak antique radio landslide accident, his body found weeks later by a neighbour complaining of the smell.

Con: Kate grows up an orphan; with no moral direction, she takes up a career in adult entertainment and renames herself Summer Rain.

Pro: You can pass Poncho, the family inheritance, onto your so-deserving sister.

The practically prepubescent salon attendant suggests that perhaps you are slightly "too paranoid" to tan here, and says she would appreciate it if you did not "freak out" the other customers in line, who now mumble to each other about the likelihood of the bed locking while the bulbs continue to fry their skin. She firmly suggests buying a "self-tanning product." She also firmly suggests a lifetime ban from Sun Spot Tanning Salon. Perhaps a bit too firmly.

"Indoor tanning isn't for everyone," she says, making lying motionless in a bed for fifteen minutes sound like going to med school or becoming a mother.

6

Get Your Groove Back (or Whatever You Had Before That Might Pass as a Groove—A Really Charming Rut, Maybe?)

Pick up the first bottle of self-tanner you see at the drugstore down the street from the gym. A generic-looking blonde in a white bikini promises you a "natural-looking, bronzed glow." Do you want to "glow"? You associate someone who "glows" with someone who has fallen into a vat of radioactive waste, or someone who is pregnant, though not a single person described you as "glowing" back when you were pregnant with Kate (mostly they used the words "teen," "knocked up," and "haven't you ever heard of protection?"). However, looking "bronzed" sounds nice, as does looking "natural." You also consider buying a nicotine patch, but before you can make it to that aisle you calculate that a cigarette would improve your current situation by a million percent. Majority rules.

You pull into the driveway five minutes later. You light a second cigarette on your way from the car to the house. Kate meets you at the back door with a purring Poncho in her arms. You wonder how Kate could possibly support a cat that weighs at least five hundred pounds, and how much wet cat food Kate must have fed him in order to elicit purring from a cat who normally only breaks his silence to pass gas. Kate begins rubbing her face against Poncho's and yet does not gag from the smell of his breath. She must be suffering from a serious sinus infection, complete nasal cavity blockage.

"Mother," Kate says, "I really think you should stop smoking, it isn't healthy—"

"I know, I—"

"For Poncho to breathe secondhand smoke all day," Kate continues. "Oh, and Jerry called. He wants you to call him back."

You wonder why Jerry would call after you just spoke to him at the gym. Your heart feels as if it has congealed inside your body. Is there such thing as heart cancer? You should've picked up that nicotine patch. In other news, if cats could fake-cough that's what Poncho would be doing right now.

*

To make Jerry think you have a life, wait until 7:30 that evening to return his call. Don't leave a message.

*

With Ben away teaching his night class, strip down in your bedroom, pop open your golden pancake paint, and slather it on every epidermal surface you can reach. You're brainstorming ways of applying the tanner to your back (the best option so far: taping a sponge to a backscratcher), when you hear Kate in the hallway.

"Kate, Honey. Can you come in here and rub some self-tanner on my back?"

"Are you naked?"

"Maybe... " You stare at your naked breasts and slightly protruding lower belly in the mirror. Your top belly, however, is in great shape.

"Gross!" You might agree with her, but your back still looks like the iridescent parts of sliced ham.

"You came out of my goddamn uterus, Kate. You're the one who stretched out my lower belly when you were a selfish fetus kicking your selfish fetus feet. Now get in here!"

"I thought the bodies of teen moms were supposed to bounce right back!" she yells.

You hear her run up the stairs. Fine. You tend to wear shirts anyhow; no one has to see your back. The rest of your skin already browning up and feeling Fruit Roll-Up sticky. To dry yourself, begin skipping around your room, violently backstroking and jumping-jacking.

Three thoughts occur to you as you interpretive dance in the buff:

1. You really have done a lot of physical activity today.

2. You deserve to reward yourself with two or three Oreo cookie sleeves.

3. You should probably close the blinds.

- -

*

When Ben gets home from work that night he does not immediately compliment you on your sun-kissed glow.

Instead he says, "Carrie, I don't want to offend you, but your face looks a little... well, dirty." He says you might want to wash it. The blonde in the white bikini did not warn you about looking dirty. You run to the mirror affixed to the hallway wall. Your face now features "natural-looking, bronzed" zebra stripes.

"It's just that stupid self-tanner," you say, your hands frantically rubbing your cheeks. Ben takes this as his cue to erupt into a fit of his signature dolphin laughter, which has become increasingly less endearing since the first time you witnessed it.

"Kate, get down here and look at your mother!"

Predictably Poncho also comes to point and laugh, which he does by sitting motionless at your feet.

You manage to escape to the bathroom before your loving family decides they must ship you off to the care of Barnum and Bailey to take your rightful place next to the bearded lady. You should've faked leprosy. If under your sink you find one of the following items: (a) rubbing alcohol, (b) hydrogen peroxide, (c) make-up remover, or (d) nail polish remover, then you don't have enough chemically-based cleaning products— you'll need to go to the store to collect the other three items.

Fifteen minutes of scrubbing and you've made great strides towards un-zebra-ing yourself—enough that you could be convinced to go out into a public place with very poor lighting. On the down side, every one of your skin cells are now just kindle for the bonfire that is your face.

*

"How do you do it?" you ask Tina, 9:00 PM Mountain Standard Time (MST), 11:00 PM Time Zone That Actually Matters (TZTAM). Ben is upstairs, in your bedroom, laptop on his crotch, squinting at the screen. When you crawled into bed next to him, began to massage his shoulders, and asked him if he needed a break, he responded with a simple "no."

"Huh?" Tina asks and yawns into the phone. You can hear the television in the background, the laugh-track of some sitcom rising and falling in waves.

"Seduce your husband. Make Vince want you. You know, put him in the mood." You half-watch your own sitcom, the volume turned down, characters seemingly doing nothing but gesticulating wildly at each other.

"Hell if I know," Tina says, yawns again. "We haven't had sex in at least a month." Why has Tina never mentioned this before?

"But you have the bosom of an Elizabethan oil painting and the shiny, flaxen hair of Gwyneth Paltrow! If you aren't getting any, there's no hope for any of us."

"Yeah well, being a parent is exhausting," she says like she's speaking to her younger, childless sister. "Honestly, I don't even miss it. Last time we did it, Vin kept his socks on, I was wearing this hideous sweatshirt and watching *Saturday Night Live* over his shoulder, we didn't even kiss or make eye contact, and I just felt sad that I was missing sleep for this."

"Okay, but what do you think I should do? About Ben?"

"I dunno, Carrie. Can we talk later? I have to frost three dozen cupcakes and wash my flaxen hair."

You hang up, turn up the volume. Kate walks in, asks you to turn it down.

"Some of us don't have the luxury of watching TV all night," she says.

You tell her about a long, stressful, fictional day at work. So many accounts needed counting!

"I just need to turn my brain off," you say.

*

On the seventh day of your sabbatical Ben confronts you as soon as you open the back door.

"Carrie, come in here. I need to talk to you." He's chopping some sort of purple vegetable in the kitchen. Either eggplant or cabbage (or maybe a turnip? a rutabaga? bok choy? You're no vegetable connoisseur). He stops chopping to meet you at the back door. Arms crossed—though vegetable cleaver still in hand—he makes that face where he looks like he's swallowing his own lips. You knew you were coming home prematurely and should've driven around the block a couple of times, but you can always tell him you ducked out of work early. You apparently had a habit of doing that.

"Is there some news you want to share?" You really wish he'd put the large knife down on the cutting board while you have this conversation.

"News? I'm not sure that I know what you're talking about—"

"C'mon Carrie, I've been thinking about it for days and now I've got it!"

While his enthusiasm over the loss of your job rather puzzles you, his brandishing the knife around like that starts to give you Vietnam flashbacks (i.e., that time Jerry made you watch *Platoon*).

Play dumb, flip to page 102.

"And what exactly do you 'got'?"

"You got that raise, didn't you?"

"What?" You are no longer playing dumb.

"The raise you told me you planned to ask your boss for. You got it, didn't you? That's why you've been in such a good mood for the past couple days?" He puts down the knife and wipes his hands on the front of his pants. His lips reemerge from his mouth un-swallowed. You force your anus to unclench.

"I have?"

"Completely. You've even been nicer to Poncho!"

"????"

"Yeah, I knew something was up. You've been so happy, like a new and improved Carrie!" He puts his arms around your middle and squeezes. Your arms hang limp at your sides.

Don't bother asking why it was that you needed improving. Just accept the upgrade.

Whatever you do, don't blurt out a marriage proposal.

"Do you want to get married?" you ask.

- -

Things You Would Expect Ben to Say When You Accidentally Proposed to Him

1. "Did you just start your period?"

2. "Seth fired you, didn't he?"

3. "Are you sure you want to make such a major life change so soon after the funeral? You're in a very vulnerable state right now."

4. "The purple bottle of pills is for Poncho's heart, not for your hangovers."

- -

What Ben Actually Said When You Accidentally Proposed to Him:

1. "City Hall, or something bigger?"

- -

Like clockwork, immediately after you accidentally propose to Ben, Kate returns from walking Poncho who is both leashed and purring, though you adamantly warned her against spending her babysitting money on a cat-leash for a haughty, melodramatic cat. Kate and Poncho (still leashed) both saunter, noses in air, to the living room, while you whisper to Ben that Kate and Poncho have been ganging up on you.

"Poncho's having a bad influence on her."

"Yeah, I should have a word with him about his smoking and his drinking in front of your daughter."

*

Later, you catch Poncho deriding your cooking ability from atop the kitchen counter while you attempt to prepare a wholesome dinner, the likes of which you've deprived your family all week because you've been "just too damn swamped at work" to have time for anything but Chinese takeout and pizza. You start to wonder if there will ever come a good time to tell Ben and Kate that you were fired. A week ago.

Ben moseys up beside you while you stand over the stove, puts his mouth next to your ear, and in a whisper you can only assume he means to be romantic, asks if you are making a "celebration dinner." You lose your appetite. Poncho makes a sound you assume to be cat laughter.

*

During dinner, Kate complains about the dryness of her pork chop and the runny-ness of her mashed potatoes.

Say: "At least it's not the other way around, huh?"

No one finds this funny.

Ben clears his throat and announces without warning, "Kate, your mother and I have some important news to share."

Your runny mashed potatoes somehow configure themselves into a hard clump at the back of your throat which prevents you from breathing. As you gasp for air you hear Poncho purring wildly.

Perhaps your choking might distract Ben from announcing accidental wedding plans to your daughter, so although your airways are now as clear as your day planner, begin waving your arms frantically and grunt the word "choking" in Neanderthal without opening your mouth. Now would be a good moment to fake your own death.

Ben jumps up from the table and rushes to your side with his glass of water and begins pounding—pounding—on your back. Kate chirps "Give her the Heimlich!" too enthusiastically, clearly interested not in its lifesaving properties but its sheer entertainment value. As Ben wraps his arms around you, about to break a rib or two, you figure he has been sufficiently red-herringed to announce any "important news" to Kate. You're also sure Kate won't bother asking about the news. He did say it was "important" after all. So begin breathing quickly, reassuring them, through artificially deep, spastic breaths, that you're now fine. Take several sips of water, and pretend to get your breathing back on track to prove that you do not, in fact, require the Heimlich.

Kate prods her potatoes wearily like you might have poisoned them but weren't smart enough to steer clear of them yourself. You see her smirk at Poncho. Ben, not missing a beat, says, "Kate, as I was saying, we have some important news for you. I think you'll be really excited to know—"

"We're taking you to Disney World!" you exclaim.

You hate Disney World. You have always hated Disney World. The one activity you and your mother enjoyed together was joint-hating Disney World. You hate no place on the planet as much as you hate Disney World, with the exception, of course, of Disneyland. But if you know Kate, you know that Kate would never want to go to Disney World. Unless, of course, it was the EuroDisney in Paris (Kate has told you on many occasions that she wishes she had been born to Parisian art dealers). You prepare to be ridiculed for being "ultra family sitcom lame," a fate you would today gladly accept, when she says, "Okay. Can An-DREY-uh come with us?"

You haven't seen her look at you like this in a long time, possibly since you could win her affection by buying her Chicken NcNugget Happy Meals.

"Sure she can. The more the merrier!" you say somehow, though you haven't opened your mouth. Don't reach a hand to Ben. Instead, busy yourself rearranging the food on your plate and wondering where you are possibly going to come up with the money for a vacation now that your savings account has been squandered at Joe Mama's.

"When do we leave?" Kate draws her cell phone from the pocket of her thrift store cardigan. You wonder if she always brings her cell phone to the dinner table. Has she been secretly recording you? Putting it up on YouTube?

"Oh, not for..." You begin, thinking of finishing the sentence with "a lifetime," when Kate's face sags like a wet paper bag. What Tinkerbell-loving demon has replaced your daughter at your dinner table?

"Well, let's say... soon..." you say, hoping you will never have to define "soon." Might Kate be onto you? Perhaps she is calling your bluff. That, or she's been taking some seriously mind-altering drugs. Ones that will need to be confiscated. And experimented with. To ensure no lasting damage. On Kate's brain.

As soon as she leaves the dining room, Ben hisses, "Disney World? What's going on, Care?"

You don't answer, because you can't answer; you have stupefied even yourself. You begin clearing the table, chiseling away with a butter knife at all your uneaten, possibly fatal, mashed redskin potatoes, flinging them into the garbage can under the sink.

"I mean, I love Disney World, but..."

Of course Ben loves Disney World. His heart pure and innocent as Snow White's and equally naïve. How did he survive without you? Take the other day, for instance: you had to swoop in and save him from those two cult members dressed like Girl Guides on your front porch trying to dupe him into handing over his credit card number. Thankfully, you had been to an ATM that day and had enough cash to purchase two boxes of Thin Mints and two boxes of Lemon Chalet Cremes.

Poor Ben. You picture him wearing a fanny pack, tube socks, and running shoes, maybe even one of those mouse-ear-hats. He would be even more excited than Kate and An-DREY-uh to ride in a giant, bright pastel teacup. They would spin and laugh and yell for you to take their picture while you hold everyone's bags and souvenirs and sport a bad sunburn because Tanning Salon Girl—barely older than the baby on the bottles of Coppertone—banned you from getting that base tan, standing with the expectant (and naturally glowing) mothers behind the metal gate that doesn't look strong enough to protect anyone should a teacup spontaneously derail. Undoubtedly, you will feel an encroaching wave of nausea from merely watching the spiraling tea-cup-shaped death machines through the viewfinder of your digital camera.

"Seriously, Care? You want to go to Disney World?" Apparently, he doesn't want to pretend this whole conversation never happened.

Choose not to answer. Who knows what might come out of your mouth should you open it?

Ben gingerly packs up the leftovers into Tupperware containers though he must know that what was barely edible tonight will be completely unfit for human consumption tomorrow.

"Why didn't you want to tell Kate we're getting married?"

Silence.

"What's going on, Carrie?"

Silence.

"You can't never speak to me again."

You have started to feel like (a) a dead body that Ben is poking with a stick and (b) seventeen again sitting on your couch at two in the morning as your father asks you where you were all night, who you were with, and why you smell like booze and cigarettes.

Well, Father Dearest, I didn't actually make it to the bowling alley, and I didn't really just "hold" a cigarette for a friend, and the punch didn't really get "spiked without my knowledge." I was severely intoxicated and thought it might be fun to climb into the back of Matthew's parents' station wagon to conceive a child. You remember Matt, don't you? You don't? Neither do I, really. Oh, and by the way, you and mom get a divorce in two years and you die of a heart attack in six.

You have no intention of answering Ben when words begin to stream from your mouth like drool does whenever you fall asleep on public transportation.

"I thought we could have one of those destination weddings, you know? Like get married in Cinderella's castle or something? Don't they do that there?" You hear these words come out of your mouth but don't remember thinking them.

"Sure, if that's what you want... but why not tell Kate? I mean, I feel like we've been getting along ..." Ben takes the pot you've been holding in your motionless hands, hovering over the sink, and begins to wash it.

"I thought that we could do one of those surprise weddings, too. Just ask everyone to come take a vacation and then all of a sudden we're at the altar! Surprise! I thought about not even telling you, ha ha."

"Don't you think you should at least run it by Kate?"

"No! I mean, you never let the maid of honour in on the surprise. If you're going to tell anyone, it can't be the maid of honour."

Suddenly you are Surprise Destination Weddings for Dummies. Have you seen some sort of television special about them recently? On the Food Network perhaps?

"That's sweet, Carrie, but how will we pay for this? There's the wedding... then the vacation part? And Andrea? I thought you didn't even like Andrea, and now you want to bring her on a trip? To our wedding?"

"Yeah, well, I want Kate to have someone there when we wanna—y'know— be alone." You give him an overly dramatic wink and suddenly feel like a cast-member on some reality show, *Wife Swap* or *Common-Law Partner Switch-Up*. You are playing yourself and doing a terrible job.

"Well, you did get that raise. That'll help. Sorry, here you are planning this elaborate Surprise-Destination-Wedding surprise, and I'm harping on about the cost. If you really want to do this, we'll make it happen."

Oh yes, the raise. If you had not already thrown away all traces of your attempt at mashed potatoes, you would stuff them down your throat and hope to really choke on their red skins. You decide you need something that will cheer you up; accordingly you decide now sounds like the perfect time for Poncho's biweekly bubble bath.

Things Poncho Would Do if He had Opposable Thumbs

1. Call both your ex-husband and ex-boss on a conference call so they could congratulate each other on abandoning the sinking ship of your life. He would kindly put the call on speaker phone so you could listen in.

2. Tell Ben about the time you were so overcome with terror riding Disney World's Splash Mountain that you peed your pants and claimed the spot on your pants—in the shape of a thought bubble emerging from your crotch like it had a great idea—was just water from the "Splash," though Jerry and nine-year-old Kate knew better.

3. Make himself a bologna sandwich.

4. Murder you in your sleep.

Things Poncho Is Doing Because He Is a Cat:

1. Taking a bubble bath.

2. Trying to simultaneously amputate your limbs and scalp you.

3. Wishing he had opposable thumbs so he could make a bologna sandwich after he murders you in your sleep.

- -

Giving Poncho a bath has put you in such a good mood you figure you can stomach calling Jerry again—at least once you've fortified your stomach with a glass of Pinot, a cold hot dog, and a shot of Pepto-Bismol.

"Hello?" A woman's voice.

You hang up. You have much experience hanging up on people who have called you but since you haven't been to many sixth-grade slumber parties recently, this hang-up feels a bit foreign. The phone rings before you can completely set it back in the cradle. Is calling and hanging up illegal? Maybe the police have traced your call.

"Hello?"

"Hi, Carrie." At least it's Jerry and not his croissant-baking hussy.

"Jerry, what a pleasant surprise!" Light a cigarette and tell your stomach to play it cool. Threaten it with another shot of the pink stuff if necessary.

"You just called me."

"No I didn't." You hope he can hear you smoking.

"Then you hung up."

"Preposterous!"

"You do realize I have Caller ID?" Caller ID, how you miss Caller ID! Ben cancelled it from your service when he realized having Caller ID meant you never answered the phone (see pie chart of people who call your landline).

"Maybe a pocket-dial?"

"From your landline?"

"They do make them cordless these days, you know. Perfect for keeping in your pocket while cleaning the house."

"Oh, your cleaning day! Must be the second Sunday of the fourth month. Should I call back when you have more time?"

Waiting for your ex-husband to call back sounds even less fun than talking to your ex-husband.

"It's fine, go ahead."

"Go ahead and call you back later?"

Anyone who enjoys talking on the phone should be entitled to a free psych evaluation.

What Jerry will eventually tell you: the woman who answered the phone is now expecting Jerry's child, Jerry and this woman plan to get married (though somehow this wedding is not a "shotgun" wedding and the suggestion of such is offensive), and Jerry would like to introduce this woman to your child.

"The woman from the gym?"

"Yes, that's where we met actually."

"The woman from the gym is pregnant? How is that even possible? No way there's a baby in there. Unless she's pregnant with a drawing of a baby on a sheet of paper. She's trying to trick you! Trap you into marriage! Is she trying to get a green card? Did you go to the ultrasound with her? They can fake those photos, you know."

Jerry doesn't appreciate your concern.

"We're so happy. Over the moon."

"Too bad not literally."

He tells you he wants to maintain his relationship with Kate, doesn't want to keep this information from her, so can she come over for dinner?

"Look, yeah, me too," you tell him.

"Sorry, you want to come for dinner too?"

"No, no, I mean, I'm really happy too. And I'm actually getting married again myself. Ben and I have planned an elaborate and very expensive Destination Wedding in Disney World, Cinderella's castle, the works. So yeah, introduce Kate to whoever you want. Listen, I'd love to chat but I've got to meet with the caterer tonight and do extensive taste-testing. So busy with wedding plans!"

"How can you meet with the caterer if it's in Disney World? And you hate that place. Remember when you peed yourself on Splash Mountain?"

"Like I said, really busy. Got to go."

*

The next day, your sister calls while you're in your office (re: Joe Mama's Coffee House) watching YouTube clips on the new widescreen laptop you bought with your severance pay.

"A Surprise Destination Wedding, Carrie? So unlike you—I love it! I've already called the people at Cinderella's castle, but some bad news: there aren't any openings for almost five years. How do you feel about Snow White?"

"She was a little polygamous, don't you think? Even for you? I mean seven men—"

"You could still be a princess in Snow White's cottage, and they have an opening in a couple months. What do you think?"

"Izzy! I think it's not a surprise anymore, so better just cancel the whole thing. Darn! Besides, how could I ever decide who's going to marry us: Sleepy or Sneezy?"

"Doc is the obvious choice and we can still surprise everyone else. No one knows except me and I'm apparently not the maid of honour so no big deal. I understand. I'm really not upset... Well, I was a teensy bit hurt when I first found out, but Kate is your daughter. So fine. I mean, it's—"

"Izzy, please. I can't believe you even know about this. Do you have Jerry on speed dial? 'Cause you really should have warned me that he's expecting."

"Expecting what?"

"Company. In the form of a baby."

"Jerry's having a baby? Okay, I'm confused, why would he know about your wedding?"

Don't answer that. "So, then how do you know about the wedding?"

"Ben, obviously. He called me this morning because he knows how you hate organizing these things and you would leave it 'til the last minute and it—"

"Oh really? I'm terrible at organizing surprise destination weddings in Disney World? Funny, I don't remember ever organizing one before. Must have slipped my mind because it was so awful." You wonder what's getting you so worked up about a wedding that obviously can't happen regardless who plans it.

"Carrie, c'mon, you know what we mean." Your boyfriend and your sister have somehow transmuted themselves into a cohesive, thought-sharing "we." Make a note to buy the two of them a tandem bicycle for Christmas.

"I dunno, Iz, I actually didn't mean to—"

"Also, it's funny 'cause Ben mentioned something about you getting a raise at work. I went along with it 'cause maybe he thinks I don't know work let you go, but he knows... obviously."

"Why does everyone feel the need to phrase being terminated as being 'let go'?" You restart your YouTube video. A baby panda sneezes.

"Okay, if you prefer 'fired,' then you did tell him you got fired, right?"

"'Fired' sounds so harsh. I guess I do prefer 'let go.'"

"Carrie!"

You begin biting the nail of your right index finger.

"Carrie!!"

Switch to the middle finger.

"Carrie!!!"

Pinky finger.

"If you weren't planning to tell him you got fired, why would you tell him you got a raise? That's insane! So, what? Reality has no place in your life anymore?"

Try to decide on the next video from the sidebar of suggested videos: Epic Funny Cats Compilation, Goat Screaming Like a Human, Babies Scared of Farts.

"I dabble in reality from time to time."

"My God! It's not scrapbooking or water aerobics!"

"Well, television has given it such a bad name lately."

"What the hell is that noise? Is someone screaming over there? It sounds like you just told a sick orphan you're going to be his new mommy."

You mark this as the most appropriate time to hang up the phone: your nails at the quick, you'll have to make a snack-run at the very least. Two minutes later a new email chimes from your inbox. From: Izzy. The subject line reads: "Get your act together. Stop lying. Don't be such a fetus." You delete the email without opening it. Likely Izzy did not even write anything in the body of the email—she knows you well enough to put whatever she needs to say in the subject line.

*

You recognize the pointlessness of waking up at eight every morning since you are no longer a card-carrying member of the real world. You begin sleeping in until ten, eleven, noon, explaining to Ben that management is in the process of testing various start times in an effort to increase productivity. Inexplicably you also always arrive in your driveway by five every day.

"You know Seth, always trying to push the manila envelope."

Is there any way to make lying a profession? It's fast becoming your number-one asset.

--- --- --- --- --- --- --- --- --- --- --- --- --- --- ---

Possible Careers for a Compulsive Liar With Over Sixteen Years of Experience

1. Motivational speaker on high school tour circuit.

2. Weather forecaster.

3. Representative for experimental drug company seeking approval from Health Canada. Many meetings in alcohol-serving coffee shops to contemplate whether or not you can categorize death as a side effect.

4. CEO of line of self-tanning products.

5. Writer of celebrity biographies.

6. Writer of newspaper obituraries.

7. Writer of self-help book.

- -

The next week you also forgo making yourself work-place-presentable each morning.

"The dress code? Seth finally came to his senses after I staged a naked sit-in. As long as I'm wearing any sort of clothing these days, he's happy."

Similarly, driving to the coffee shop to half-heartedly flip through the Classifieds, and whole-heartedly read the obits, loses its appeal. You convince Ben that you've gotten so far ahead in your work that Seth has agreed to let you work from home.

"Seth recognizes that I'm one of those self-motivated people who doesn't require the constant supervision and the confines of a stifling office setting." This way you will also have time to work on planning the wedding, you tell him. "And I'll finally have time to read all the wedding magazines you've been buying!"

- -

Lost: Integrity.
If Found, Please Return to: The woman in the super-market's eight-items-or-fewer line (though she has thirteen) who hesitantly picks up wedding maga-zines before being overcome by what looks like a violent bout of the stomach flu, and shoves them behind the less offensive magazines with the near-ly-naked, large-chested women on the front covers.

- -

You spend the weekend converting your den into a home office, creating the perfect place to concentrate on writing your book. It proves itself to be quite a conducive work environment (i.e., your FreeCell statistics instantly improve). 89% to win.

*

You call Tina at 9:30 PM MST, 11:30 PM TZTAM.

"Hey," you say, "Be honest and tell me what you think of Ben. Honestly. What you really think."

"It's just Carrie," she whisper-yells to Vince. You hear him state what time it is as if you're calling at four a.m. on a Monday rather than eleven-thirty on a Thursday night, which is practically the weekend.

"He's so smart and nice and even-tempered, you know? I like that. The same mood every day, and so dependable. I always know where he'll be—at my house mostly, cause that's where he lives. So it makes sense that he would be here all the time. I mean apparently he has an office at the college, but it's fine that he'd rather work from home. Because my home is his home. I mean he is paying half the rent."

"Mm, sure, he sounds really sweet, Care."

"Maybe he's too sweet?"

"I'll tell you to break up with him if you want me to."

"Why? Do you think he's not the one for me?"

"Carrie, I have no fucking clue. I met the guy once. Sorry." She says "sorry" as if she is asking for an apology rather than giving one.

*

When Ben comes home Monday evening he says he has some "news."

"I can't wait to tell you, but it's so good I almost think I should save it for a special occasion, like date night." He joins you in the living room where you've been flipping through television channels for so long your clicker thumb has developed new muscles. He has yet to take off his coat. You don't remember ever scheduling a "date night" with Ben.

"That's perfectly fine. Let's wait until Christmas. I don't know how much more 'news' I can handle." Speaking of which, there are far too many news channels. You wonder if Ben took it upon himself to order some special world news cable package.

"You're not at all curious?" he pouts.

"Nope! I will wipe my brain clear of the fact that you are sitting on potentially catastrophic news and not tell me for months. There is still some wine left, isn't there? That should do the trick." You head for the kitchen.

"Christmas? How about a romantic dinner?" you suggest. He follows you.

"What's more romantic than Christmas dinner? With the whole family? Of course, my mother won't be able to attend this one." You actually manage one tear—your tear ducts apparently not paralyzed after all, even if you do have to squeeze the moisture out with the force you imagine is required to milk an almond.

"Okay, I'm going to just go ahead and tell you." Such a great listener, that Ben.

"I'll give you Thanksgiving." You take out a bottle of white wine.

"I'm just too excited. I—"

"Fine, Labour Day. Can it wait until Labour Day?" You edge past him to the drawer where you keep all your tools. Inside: a rusty can opener, a bottle opener, and three corkscrews.

"You know how I've always been really interested in art?"

"No, I thought Kate was the only abstract grey-scale painter in this house. Do we have a holiday in August? You could save it for—"

"Well, you know how I'm always drawing, doodling all over anything I can get my hands on?" You viciously stab the cork.

"Um." What would Ben doodle? Probably something symmetrical, drawn to proportion using formulas and rulers.

"The first of July is only a few months away. You could tell me during a firework show." The cork pops its way out of the bottle. "How special would that be?"

"Care, listen: I think I need to take a more creative path in life."

"Teaching art at the community college is a great idea! Knock yourself out!" You squeeze past him to the cabinet and take out your favourite mug. A square giraffe whose neck is the handle.

"You're not listening, Carrie."

"Well, I was under the impression you were going to wait until—"

"I want to make art my full-time profession." You put the mug back in the cabinet and raise the bottle to your mouth. So thirsty.

"Just out of curiosity, how many organs does one actually need to remain living, per se? My liver might only be worth a buck-twenty-five but I bet one of my kidneys would fetch a handsome profit."

"I wouldn't seriously think about quitting teaching if it wasn't for your work bonus. We can live off your salary until my painting career takes off."

"My, um, work bonus?" So very thirsty.

"Izzy just called me on my way home from work to tell me the great news. First the raise, then the bonus. Congratulations, Employee of the Year!" Not enough wine in the world.

"Just out of curiosity, does this mean that the college might put out a call for a new math teacher?"

"I guess they'll start looking after this semester."

"And are they dead set on hiring someone with a math degree, or is there some flexibility with that?"

*

1999: the year both you and your mother had respective buns in your respective ovens: yours a long-limbed fetus you would name Kate, your mother's a group of rapidly multiplying cells she would name Herbie. You did not know about Herbie. She did not know about Kate. You guarded your respective buns with respective fervour.

"Carrie, I'm a little concerned." Your mother said one day during Jeopardy!'s second commercial break. Your mother watched Jeopardy! not because she was remotely adept at trivia but because shouting insults at Alex Trebek in the form of questions rejuvenated her spirits in a way that a brisk walk or a cup of tea might for someone more sane than she.

You crossed your arms, lacing them through the front pocket of your oversized hooded sweatshirt, guarding your stomach in a way that had become habit. At least your father was out somewhere getting drunk and forgetting he had a family. Maybe you could convince your mother to keep your secret from him. Maybe he would never come out of his vodka-induced stupor long enough to even notice a diapered baby scampering around on his oriental carpets.

"There's no easy way to say this, so I'm just going to say it: you look fat. Real fat. Especially in the middle. Frankly, you look like one of my garden gnomes. The specially pudgy one. You know the one with the blue overalls? The one I named Mervin. Well, you—"

"Really, Mother? There's no easier way to say that? Pick a euphemism for 'fat.' Any one. Chubby, big-boned, husky..."

You wanted out of your husky, pregnant body, wished you could freaky-Friday with Izzy away attending a liberal arts college, majoring in women's studies and studying women. You would have even settled for a strict Christian college, the classes taught by Jesuits who had taken lifelong vows of silence. Or clown college. Or one of those seedy barely-college colleges they advertise for during late-night TV that will prepare you for something practical like medical administration but your diploma might arrive printed on the back of a Chinese takeout menu and your major might be listed in quotation marks. Or the college that trains you for a career as a hairdresser, a park ranger, a psychic. Anywhere but with your mother.

"I'm just looking out for your well-being. That's what mothers do. They tell their daughters when they look like they've shoved a pork roast up their blouse. Maybe you need to cut back on the burgers and the chili cheese dogs. Get out for a brisk walk. Watch less TV."

"How many times do I have to tell you that I'm a vegetarian?!" you shouted on your way to the pantry to grab a bag of Cheetos, which you shook like a tambourine up the stairs to your room.

"Who are people with higher IQs than Alex Trebek?" From your bedroom you heard your mother settling into Double Jeopardy. You thought about congratulating her on becoming a Grandma after she awarded herself a Daily Double for "What are things Alex Trebek has suppressed deep within his subconscious?" But then you chickened out and instead began doing crunches on your bedroom floor, rewarding yourself with Cheetos for abdominal crunches in a ratio of 2:1.

*

You fall asleep thinking about the months you spent alone in your bedroom, furiously doing abdominal exercises even though you could no longer find evidence of muscles no matter how hard you poked. In a dream, you give birth to Kate, who emerges from the womb a fully formed sixteen-year-old, permanently folded in half at the hips, her face the colour of Cheeto dust. Covered in embryonic fluid, she's yelling at you, blaming you for her bad posture and the kids at school who chase her around calling her Carrot Face and Oompa Loompa.

- -

Fact: Oompa Loompas have been fighting for a workers' union since 1971.

- -

You wake to a scratching noise below your headboard and check the bedside clock. 9:03. Your alarm isn't set to go off until noon. You reach for Ben's therapeutic foam pillow and smother yourself with it. You can still hear the scratching.

"Poncho! Quit that or it's dry cat food for a week!"

The noise stops. Then starts, stops, starts again.

"Poncho, I mean it! What are you clawing at?" you ask, before realizing that Poncho is hogging the covers and, contrary to the laws of physics, occupying more of the bed than you. For some reason your mind goes from Poncho to a radioactively enlarged cockroach as the culprit of the scratching noise. Hoist Poncho up around the belly and lower him behind the headboard to investigate. A vicious brown something scurries across the hardwood and disappears into your closet.

"Sic it, Poncho!" you scream, now standing tiptoe on your duvet, pointing to your closet as if Poncho could see you. As if Poncho could see you and ever responded to any of your commands. As if Poncho ever took a break from impersonating an elderly sloth with arthritis to partake in any form of physical exertion.

"Good for you, Fatty. You just missed your breakfast."

- -

"What to do About Mice in Your House"
Written by: Various Internet Bloggers

1. "Buy mousetraps. The humane trap detains the mouse inside, but does not kill it. You will then have to release it into the wild, like out in the suburbs (where it will most likely find its way back into your house) or remove the mouse from the humane trap to kill it yourself. Common ways to kill mice that have been caught in humane traps

are with a hammer, by drowning, or by suffocation in a plastic bag. Another type of mouse trap is the snap trap which is supposed to the kill the mouse the moment it contacts the spring, but these often go wrong, leaving a partially dead mouse with one limb snapped open. Again, you may have to use the hammer, the bucket of water, or the plastic bag."
Posted by: DrX

2. "Buy mouse poison. Mouse poison comes in the form of blocks or small, clear plastic bags filled with pellets. Place the poisonous bait near suspected nests and feeding areas. When ingested, the poison should kill the mouse after one to twenty feedings. The poisoned mouse will then find a place to die, typically in the nest, usually located inside the wall. The decaying mouse carcass will only smell for a few weeks, but may be especially pungent if the mouse has died in close proximity to a vent. Poisonous mouse bait should not be used in a house with small children or pets, as the poison is potentially fatal for them as well."
 Posted by: DrX

3. "Get a cat. Preferably one that is not overweight and lazy with a cataract in one eye. You may want to check its background to ensure that its mother was an avid mouse-hunter. Also, spoiled cats will often feel that mouse-hunting is beneath them, so you will want to avoid catering to your cat's every plea for more teri-yaki-flavoured beef jerky. If your cat is already spoiled

try not giving it food for a few days. That should renew its fighting spirit!"
Posted by: KATLOVAH

4. "Forget the expensive traps and poisons. I have a solution that works every time and uses what you have lying around your house. Here's what you do. First get an old bathtub. Place it where you know the mice like to spend their time. Fill it half-full with water. Get a strong wire and attach its ends to each side of the bathtub so that the wire runs taut, lengthwise across the top of the tub. Now wrap a slice of processed cheese around the wire in the middle and coat the wire in bacon grease. Lured by the smell of bacon and cheese, the mouse will climb up the tub to the wire and run across to the cheese. The bacon grease will cause the mouse to slip into the water where it will drown in less than an hour. Every morning I wake up to five or six drowned mice in the bathtub. It's great! As easy as bobbing for apples!"
Posted by: MOUSEGRINDR

5. "Place saucers filled with fizzy, sugary soda around mice feeding areas. The mice will drink the soda for the sugar and then literally explode from the carbonation. Kind of messy, I admit, but works every time!"
Posted by: TINKERBEL9

6. "Or just grill them."
Posted by: GuyWhoReallyLikesBalloons

- -

How do you deal with the recent infestation of your house by filthy rodents? Call a costly exterminator, flip to page 74.

Buy cheap mousetraps from Dollar Town, turn to page 56. Decide it is time for Poncho to begin a week-long fast in order to get him nice and hungry for the mouse hunting business, proceed to page 2.

Take a break from working in your home office (i.e., reading a Wikipedia article on house mice) to have a cigarette. While enjoying your company-approved-and-encouraged smoke break, Izzy calls for the fourth time. Unlike the three other times, you decide not to press "ignore."

"Iz, I think there might be mice in my house."

"Why do you think that?"

"My horoscope warned me a mouse infestation was on the horizon."

"Seriously?"

"No, Iz. I saw one."

"What did it look like?"

"I dunno, typical mouse. Big black ears, gloved hands, red shorts—"

"Oh, funny. Is this your way of telling me something about your Disney World wedding? How fun! Let me try to guess... Okay so something about your wedding and Mickey Mouse... Let's see here—"

"Yes, I've decided on a new locale—The Mickey Mouse House has everything I've ever dreamed of in a second-wedding venue. Where better for that cute, cozy, cottage vibe we're craving? The bridesmaids can dress up as Mouseketeers and—"

"So it's not about Mickey Mouse and your wedding?"

"I can't believe this conversation is dragging on so long."

"You're eating Oreos by the sleeve in bed, aren't you?"

"C'mon, my Oreo period ended weeks ago. Critics predict my Chips Ahoy! period to be my greatest legacy."

"Leaving glasses of Diet Mountain Dew on the floor?"

"That's actually a pretty effective extermination method. The carbonation—"

"Hoarding Gummi Bears under your pillow in case you wake up in the middle of the night and need a sugar fix to carry you back into dreamland?"

"You know me so well, but no."

"Huh. I'm surprised that with Poncho around you're having this problem. I thought even the smell of a cat drives mice away. Mom certainly never had to worry about mice."

"Well, I *have* been bathing Poncho."

"He smells *that* bad?"

"I've sorta been using bathing more as a disciplinary tactic."

"Maybe if you treated him better, he'd be more inclined to do you favours."

"I'm not asking for *favours*. I am simply expecting him to follow his instinctual nature! I can't have Ben finding out that my house has a mouse infestation. He'll think I'm not clean. If he adds that to the list, it might push him over the edge, of the extremely long piece of paper he's using to write his list."

"Well, 'clean' isn't exactly a word I would use to describe you anyway. But maybe it's just that one mouse. You're probably overreacting. I'm sure it's nothing a trap won't solve. Oh, and I hope you finally told Ben you got fired once he

congratulated you on being crowned Employee of the Year."
You can almost hear your sister patting herself on the back.

You light another cigarette.

"Carrie?"

Inhale, inhale, inhale.

"Carrie?!"

*

Buy a set of three traps from Dollar Town and break two of
them after snapping your fingers inside and whaling your
hand down on the ceramic counter to free yourself. It takes
you half an hour to set the third trap, but you still have your
fingertips. Load the trap with peanut butter bait, make yourself
a peanut butter sandwich, and place the trap in the back of
your closet where you hope Ben won't later notice a rotting
mouse carcass.

The next morning, while Ben is at work, a whole litter of
mice play a game of tag on your bedroom floor. Seemingly,
the mice are no longer solely nocturnal or mind in the least
that there is a giant, hungry cat lying on the bed or that you
are shrieking profanities in your highest-pitched voice in an
attempt to match the frequency of their hearing. In other news,
later that day you find Poncho in your closet happily devouring
peanut butter off traps that double as cat feeders.

- -

The House Mouse: A Guide
Carrie F., House Mouse Expert

Characteristics
The house mouse, or Mus musculus, is a rodent of small
and slender stature with a pointed nose and virtually
hairless tail. However, its small stature does not imply

that the mouse is meek, timid, and/or non-threatening. Its eyes, beady and black, protrude from its head menacingly. House mice, usually greyish-brown with a grey or tan belly, may also vary in colour from light brown to black (black mice being an omen of imminent death). Mice can fit their bodies into tiny spaces, like cracks in walls, only one centimetre (one quarter-inch) wide, which means there is virtually no way to barricade yourself in the bathroom to sleep peacefully in your bathtub. Due to such acrobatic characteristics, house mice come in a close second to the cockroach for the title of "animal/bird/insect most likely to survive a nuclear holocaust", and are classified as an animal of "least concern" on the conservation status chart. Following their arrival on colonists' ships from Europe, house mice migrated across North America and now can be found in every province and state, including coastal areas of Alaska and every room of your home. Their droppings are black (until they eat the poisonous blocks you bought, which did not kill them but instead turned their droppings a vibrant shade of emerald), about three millimetres (0.12 inches) long, and have a strong, musty odour. Vacuuming droppings from carpeted surfaces will result in deeply satisfying clicking noises as droppings reverberate down the length of the vacuum hose; though, much like the arcade game Whack-A-Mole, the faster you vacuum the droppings, the faster the mice will produce more.

Communication
Mice, virtually colour-blind, instead rely on their keen senses of smell, touch, and hearing. Human beings hear their voices as high-pitched squeaks, but mice also

communicate with each other in the ultrasonic range, as well as through sign language and telepathy (e.g., their abilities to announce to their outdoor compatriots the wonderful food selection and nesting opportunities your house has to offer). They are also able to use their long tails like antennae to transmit warning codes amongst the mouse population.

Food Habits

House mice primarily feed on plant matter such as grain, but they will also consume human flesh, dairy products, and their own droppings (meaning you will not succeed in starving them to death). Mice usually prefer high-fat and high-protein foods, as well as sugar, even when grain and seed are present. A common meal consists of forgotten day-old restaurant mints found at the bottom of your new leather purse, feeding time demarcated by the insistent wrinkling of wrappers. An impossibly fast metabolism keeps the house mouse healthy regardless of its diet, and keeps your floors resembling the tops of chocolate-sprinkle cupcakes. Do not, however, mistake your floors for chocolate-sprinkle cupcakes, as mice droppings can carry and spread the following diseases: Hantavirus, Cholera, Influenza, Pneumonia, Yellow Fever, Hay Fever, Scarlet Fever, Rheumatic Fever, Rocky Mountain Spotted Fever, Syphilis, Tuberculosis, Meningitis, Hepatitis, and Athlete's Foot.

Activity

Mice constantly explore and learn about their environment, memorizing the locations of pathways, obstacles, food and water, shelter, and your pillow while you're sleeping. They can sense surfaces and air movements with their whiskers. Mice naturally enjoy many activities such as climbing, jumping, deactivating mouse traps, swimming, and reading minds.

When Ben gets home from work he commends you on how clean the house looks.

"I vacuumed!" you say, beaming like you've aced one of his math tests.

Ben plants a chapped-lip kiss on your forehead and calls you the "best fiancée ever." If only he knew there were green blocks of poison tucked in the corner of every closet and cupboard of the house (despite the very overt label on the box warning against using said poison blocks should you have pets). If only he knew you didn't just vacuum that morning but you spent every morning for the past four days aggressively vacuuming emerald mouse turds—instead of un-encrypting the cryptoquote and smoking the fourteenth cigarette of the day—so he wouldn't notice the potentially radioactive colony of superhuman mice invading the inner workings of your walls, waiting for the right time to feast on your brain matter.

"I want my future husband to come home to a spotless and immaculate house!" *And not think I am a feral urchin content to live in squalor among diseased vermin.*

"You're going to be home during the day tomorrow, right?"

Of course I am going to be home tomorrow. I now truly do work from home: tirelessly researching house mice and planning their demise before they can establish squatters' rights. "Yes, I'm swamped with work. I'm going to lock myself in that office all day long and— "

"Great. The exterminator will be here at eleven-thirty."

You almost think you heard the word "exterminator." Maybe it was "terminator." Yes, it is definitely more likely that a fictional Hollywood cyborg would come to your house. Maybe he can even help with the mouse problem.

"The what?"

"The exterminator I called to get rid of the mice."

"We have mice?!"

Kate walks in the back door before Ben can ask you who then land-mined the house with mouse traps and blocks of poison. Shift your attention to your favourite daughter to avoid having to answer any more mouse-related questions.

"How was your day?" you ask before she can wiggle her way out of one knee-high black leather boot.

"Since when do you care how my days are?" She shrugs out of a black leather jacket and you wonder when it was exactly that she joined a bike gang.

"What do you mean, 'Since when?' Since always. Remember last month when I asked you what you'd learned at school that day?"

She snorts.

"Humour me, Kate. How was school today? Which mother accidentally packed marijuana cigarettes into her daughter's gym bag?" Arms crossed, you bar her entrance to the dining room. Ben, standing behind you, lightly lays a hand on your shoulder.

"Maybe we should let her get settled in before we bombard her with an interrogation," Ben suggests. You should've known he'd side with Kate.

"Why does asking my daughter how her day was make me the Spanish Inquisition?"

"That's really more of an event than a thing a person can be."

"Well, you know me, I have big ambitions!"

Maybe if you pick a fight with Ben he'll forget you've inadvertently welcomed a mouse colony to inhabit your walls and then didn't warn him that he was in danger of contracting several serious diseases. Turn around to face him.

"And remind me again how many children *you've* raised?" Back to Kate. "So tell me, what happened at school today?" Your tone has lost its sing-song intonation. Poncho waddles his way between you and Kate. Great. Three against one.

"You really want to play house right now?" Kate asks, scratching Poncho between the ears to thank him for his loyalty. *Is* that what you want? To play house? Maybe some high-stakes poker, sure, but house? Definitely not. Especially since you've been playing house all week and it involves vacuuming sofa pillows and actually making use of that add-on vacuum nozzle, the one with the Tom Selleck mustache, which you had previously deemed superfluous but have since discovered it works wonders on baseboards.

"Yes, let's play functional mother-daughter. I'll be the fast-talking, hot-for-her-age Gilmore Girl and you be the fast-talking, whiny one who always wears a headband and a pout." She isn't getting off easy. You're not going to let her escape to her room to listen to Björk and write haikus on her desk with black nail polish. The two of you are going to have a mother-daughter bonding moment, goddammit.

"What do you want to hear? I had the worst day, I hate everyone, I'm dropping out. Take your pick."

Turn to Ben. "Ahh, high school. Makes you nostalgic, doesn't it?" Maybe it's a good thing her peers don't want to socialize with her. You remember that, for awhile, you were far too popular in your last months of high school…

"You wanted to hear about my day so you could mock me? Why can't you ever be a normal mom? Why did I have to get the defective mom?"

"Don't be rude. I didn't raise you to be rude."

"You're kidding, right?"

"Sorry, being serious now." You wave your hand in front of your face like it's a magic smile eraser. "What happened at school? Seriously, I want to know. Let's talk. We never talk anymore."

"Fine." Kate sighs an epic sigh, continues, "I started my period—" Ben heads to the kitchen at the mention of the "p" word. "—between second and third and had to ask my Biology teacher for a tampon— " Ben begins rummaging through the silverware drawer. "— because none of my friends will speak to me. Then I ate lunch outside—"

"A picnic!" you interrupt.

"—Alone. It was sort of raining. My hair got poufy and some idiot on the lacrosse team called me 'Poodle' and it stuck. So I'm the poodle girl now." Poncho is rubbing the length of himself against Kate's ankles and glaring up at you.

"Poodle? That's not even a clever nickname! I could think of at least three better nicknames than Poodle," you offer. She ignores you.

"Andrea accidentally elbowed me in the back on the bus and I fell into the lap of this gross ninth-grader who then pitched a tent in his pants if you know what I mean." Notice that Kate called her AN-drea, not An-DREY-uh.

"You know why I don't like camping?" Ben calls from the kitchen, "It's just too in-tents for me!"

You yell at him in the kitchen: "Oh sure, you leave the room when menstruation comes up, but she brings up erections and you're all over it?"

"Brings up!" he repeats, taking a box of pasta noodles from the cupboard. "Tell me: intentional diction choice?"

"Dick-tion! Ha! I can't think of another one—do you think you've *peaked*?"

Kate follows the two of you into the kitchen, arms crossed, clicks her tongue. "Guess we've abandoned my problems to make penis puns. Should I pretend these are going right over my head? I'm not even sure you're allowed to say the word 'penis' around your sixteen-year-old daughter. I might be obligated to call child protective services on you guys." Kate opens the refridgerator and removes a jug of Ocean Spray.

"You're only sixteen?" you fake-gasp, trying to lighten the mood. "Are you sure? Because that just does not explain the crows' feet and why your boobs sag to your knees!" You smile at Kate's flat chest. You will lift Kate's spirits with your humour.

She makes a hand-bra over her chest. "Mom!"

"Fine, what would you like to call it? A johnson? A winky? A dingle?"

"Stop it!

"A rod? A willy? A pecker?"

"Everyone at school hates me, but let's not talk about that. No, let's see how many words we can think of for 'penis.'" Kate slams her glass down hard on the kitchen counter.

"Yay, let's get some pens and paper and make a game out of it! First one to fifty?" You wink at Kate. She wrinkles her nose like she's just smelled feces, which makes sense—Poncho still circling her ankles.

"Why don't you two go play outside with the other ten-year-olds? I'll call you back in when the streetlights come on."

Ben raises his hands in a surrendering motion.

"I'm sorry, I was just trying to make you laugh. Serious time now. I swear." You put a hand on her forearm. She shakes it off, scoops Poncho up like a pile of fresh laundry, and heads for her bedroom. The Ocean Spray and empty glass remain on the counter. Her door slams for dramatic effect.

"Am I a bad mother?" you ask Ben, pouring yourself a glass of Cran Raspberry. Ben hesitates. He should not hesitate. Why did he not immediately regurgitate a litany of negative answers in a firm and serious tone?

"No... But you could have asked her why none of her friends are speaking to her." That dear, sweet Ben. Far too logical to properly deal with teenagers.

"Girls do that—go in phases, like the moon. Full moon: friends with everyone. Quarter moon: turn on your lifelong best friend. You heard she just got her period—they've probably both synced up and they were PMSing at the same time, and you know how they get at that time of the month—"

"So you're allowed to blame mood swings on PMS and if I do it, I deserve three swift kicks to the groin?"

"Yeah, pretty much," you say, hoisting yourself into sitting position on the counter where you'll have a good view of Ben making dinner. "Anyway, just watch: tomorrow they'll totes be BFFs."

"Have you been reading her text messages again?"

- -

**Text Messages from the Outbox of
Your Daughter's Cell Phone
(because the inbox was wiped clean)**

To: Jake

<<*4sure! see u @ 8*>>

To: Andrea

<<*OMG Jake just asked me to hang out 2nite!*>>

To: Andrea

<<*R U CRAZY? im obvs not gonna tell Branson!*>>

To: Andrea

<<*i dont care what she thinks... she broke up w him... like 4ever ago*>>

To: Andrea

<<*just dont say anything to her. its not like Jakes gonna tell her*>>

To: Branson

<<*no i have 2 much hmwk 2nite*>>

To: Branson

<<*ya ill see you 2morrow. goodnite xoxo*>>

To: Andrea

<<*hes not gonna find out!*>>

To: Andrea

<<*hey do u need ur parents permission to go on the pill???*>>

To: Andrea

<<*no my mom would never take me... but maybe ill ask Jerrys new gf.*>>

To: Andrea

<<*no shes cool... ill just say shes my stepmom*>>

"My daughter is a lying, cheating, teenage slut," you confess over Saturday lunch with your sister. Izzy has recently
"gone raw food" and dragged you to some new restaurant
that specializes in not cooking. She thought you'd like the
place, citing the time you "went vegetarian" while pregnant.
You remind her that your stint as a herbivore was only a
cover so you didn't have to explain to your mother why the
meatloaf you once scarfed down with a fond gleam in your
eyes now sent you reeling towards the toilet.

"What about your college vegan phase?"

"Can we get back to the Kate part?" You tried to have
this conversation with Tina but the last time you called,
she was in the ER awaiting treatment for a bite of Mitchell's
that broke the skin of her calf.

Izzy squeezes a lemon into her glass of water and then
steals the one from the rim of your glass. You nab it back.

"You could've sprung for a lemonade." You search the
menu for something with imitation bacon on it.

"Too much sugar. Plus, that's how restaurants make all
their money. Pop costs them virtually nothing. It's pretty
much just all water. Did you know that if you only order
water at restaurants you can save four hundred dollars a
year?"

"It seems like you should save more than that. Let's
see... two glasses of wine for every dinner out... at three
times a week..."

A teenage boy with the nametag Treven interrupts your
mental math to take your order. You wonder what name
Kate will give her baby when she gets knocked up. She
should count herself lucky you didn't follow your seventeen-year-old instincts and name her "Morrissey." Since

nothing on the menu seems edible, you decide to opt for a liquid lunch.

"How much money would I save per year if I only ordered drinks?"

"Taking into consideration the cost of a new liver or—"

"Kate wants to go on the pill."

"Oh my." Izzy starts trying to pick up her ice cubes with her chopsticks. "I guess it's a good thing she came to you about it."

"Not exactly."

"Carrie, what do you mean 'not exactly'?" Izzy has a habit of lowering her chin into her neck when she chastises you. She appears to be burrowing her chin into her esophagus as she taps her chopsticks on the table and waits for you to answer. You wish she was still interested in the ice cubes.

"I may have *accidentally* come across a text message or two."

Your margarita arrives with an abundance of citrus fruits decorating the rim of the glass. This might just be your healthiest meal of the week. You still don't offer Izzy a lemon slice.

"I can't believe you read her texts!" Izzy hisses before Treven moves out of earshot. He freezes in place, his head cocked in your direction. Conveniently, the table next to yours needs wiping. Very slow wiping.

"I'm the bad guy? She's the one who's sixteen and tramping it up all over town!" Treven has given up the wiping-the-table illusion altogether and now stares at you, eyes as round as lemons. You meet his stare. "You want her number? Huh? Do you?"

He turns and flees for the kitchen.

"You should take it. She'll probably do you too!" you call after him. Izzy's chin pressed so hard into her neck that she looks like she's playing that game where you have to hold an apple under your chin and pass it to a teenager of the opposite sex without dropping it.

"What's wrong with you?" Her whisper barely audible. As if being as quiet as possible could make up for your outburst.

"She's only sixteen, Iz."

Always the supportive sister, Izzy reminds you that you were pregnant at seventeen and convinced your parents you were just bloated until month seven.

"At least I wasn't two-timing the baby daddy!" Of course, as you say this, Treven has returned to drop off Izzy's plate of weeds, fungus, and squishy things. His face turns bright red, bright red and fleshy, bright red and fleshy like barbecued meat. Your stomach growls. On the bright side, Izzy's embarrassment means she might never invite you to this restaurant again.

"I know that she lies to me and that's okay—"

"It is?" Izzy knows nothing about teenagers. Not even about being one herself. She asked your mother to write "23" on her cake when she turned thirteen. She wears sunscreen in the winter. She doesn't like taking public transit because there are no seat belts. She still brings her chequebook to the bank to get it updated by the teller. She owns a complete set of encyclopedias and you have even seen her look something up in one—a perfectly fine computer with Googling capabilities mere feet away.

"Yeah, it'd be weird if she told me the truth all the time. You think I'd want to know everything? And if she's going to have sex, well okay, but not with some guy she's seeing behind her boyfriend's back. Not with a friend's ex-boyfriend."

- -

How to Talk to Your Kids About Sex

Written by: Someone, somewhere who then put it on the internet

Start Early

Teaching your children about sex demands a gentle, continuous flow of information that should begin as early as possible. (A *"gentle, continuous flow"? You can't make this stuff up.*) For instance, when teaching your toddler where each ear and toe is, include "this is your penis" or "this is your vulva" in your talks. *You envision that going over well in preschool: "Head and shoulders, knees and penis, knees and penis, knees and penis..."* Of course you'd have to change "penis" to "doodle" to get child protective services off your back.

Take the Initiative

If your child hasn't started asking questions about sex, look for a good opportunity to bring it up. Say, for instance, the mother of an eight-year-old's best friend is pregnant. You can say, "Did you notice David's mommy's tummy getting bigger? That's because she's going to have a baby and she's carrying it inside her. Do you know how the baby got inside her?" Then let the conversation move from there. *Move to where? Informing the eight-year-old what happens when* condoms break? That children grow where we digest our burritos?

Talk About More Than "The Birds and The Bees"
One aspect that many parents overlook when discussing sex with their child is dating. In movies, two people meet and later end up in bed together, whereas in real life they take the time to get to know each other—time to hold hands, go bowling, see a movie, share a root beer float, or just talk. Children need to see dating as an important part of a caring relationship.

If Kate happens to ask, you did not take Ben home to your bed immediately after meeting him in line at the grocery store. You with your cart full of organic "superfoods" like kale and sweet potatoes and pints of berries, and other "really superfoods" like Doritos and Zoodles and Diet Mountain Dew.
"Quite the mix you got there," he said, nodding into your cart.
"Oh yeah, well, that's what happens when you have a teenager to shop for," you said, not clarifying the produce was for the teenager and the junk food for you.
There were months (and months) of talking, holding hands, bowling, and float-sharing before you and Ben "ended up in bed together."
Kate never asks.

Communicate Your Values
It's your responsibility to let your children know your values about sex. Although they may not adopt these

values as they mature, at least they'll be aware of them as they struggle to figure out how they feel and want to behave. *Next step: get some values.*

Listen to Your Child
Listening to your children and taking their feelings into account also helps you understand when they've had enough. Suppose you're answering your nine-year-old's questions about diaphragms, oral sex, or AIDS *(haven't you already failed if your nine-year-old needs lessons in these topics?)*. If, after a while, he says, "I want to go out and play," stop the talk and reintroduce the subject at another time. *This must be why you've never had the talk with Kate. She must have wanted to go out play and the moment never presented itself again.*

Turn to page 78 to have "the talk" with Kate or flip to page 132 to film the delivery of the newest addition to your family.

Kate's room is upstairs next to a small bathroom and down the hall from the guest bedroom you turned into an office for Ben when he moved in; you really never had many guests, anyway. Inside, a palimpsest: posters of esoteric bands, the genre of which Kate has described to you as post-something-or-other, taped over floral wallpaper and pink paint, black clothing in heaps atop a unicorn and rainbow duvet cover, Kurt Vonnegut novels rest atop shoeboxes full of sports medals and participation ribbons. Kate's bedroom door firmly closed.

You try the knob—locked. You bought her a locking door-knob when she turned fourteen but didn't tell her you kept an extra key for "emergencies." Instead of fetching the key like you would were she not home, you knock gently. Who knows what she might be doing in there—or who.

"Kate, can I come in?" You hear rustling on the other side of the door: no doubt the rustling of a strange boy who climbed into Kate's room via the window and now tries to conceal himself as a pile of clothes in your daughter's closet. In the notepad you've been keeping on your person at all times should inspiration for your self-help book strike, you make a note to have the tree outside her window converted into toilet paper.

"One second!" she calls. More rustling. Maybe there's more than one boy in there. Or a really big boy. A really big boy who's almost a man.

It takes Kate nearly a minute to unlock the door; you know because you are counting your Mississippi's. Fifty-two. When she finally does open the door her hair is all staticky and her clothes look as though they sat in the dryer overnight.

"Kate, what were you doing in here?" You push past her and begin the investigation. You notice she relocked the window. Clever.

"Getting dressed." Kate doesn't even ask why you're on your belly looking under her bedskirt. Too busy sitting on the floor in front of her full-length mirror, tracing and retracing her eyelids with black liner.

"Of course you were getting dressed. But why were you undressed to begin with?"

Kate's reflection rolls her eyes at you, explains that she had to change for dinner at Jerry's house.

"Again? That's the second time this week," you say with your head in her closet.

"Mom, are you looking for Poncho? I really don't think he needs another bath."

"No... I actually wanted to talk to you about something." It might be easier to have this conversation without making eye contact. Correspondingly, you decide not to remove your head from the closet.

"It won't take long, will it?"

"No, no... I just wanted to talk about... well, we never really had the talk about—you know."

"Huh?" You notice Kate applies mascara just like you do. Mouth open slightly, tongue protruding, face so close to the mirror, if you were Alice, you'd have gone right through it.

"You know. The Talk. I know we had the one when you were younger, about how babies are made. I know you know how boy parts and girl parts work, but we didn't have the follow-up talk." Organize Kate's closet while you talk: shirts on one side grouped by sleeve length, bottoms on the other. Might as well keep busy in there.

"The follow-up talk?"

"Yeah, the one where I ask you if you're... active, and if you're... safe, and if you have any... questions." And why a person would need nine black T-shirts. And why are they here on hangers and not crumpled in drawers? Are these the dressy, formal black T-shirts?

"Mother, everything's fine. I'm fine. Don't worry. I know you don't want to have this conversation, so let's just not."

"No, I want to talk." Show her you're serious by getting out of the closet and sitting on her bed. An old, matted teddy bear wearing giant headphones watches you from atop a pile of pillows. You wonder if Kate still calls him Tootles.

"Okay, let's talk about my father." She sets down the tube of mascara and turns to face you.

You take Tootles onto your lap and remove his headphones.

"I will talk about him as soon as the time's right. I promise."

"Great, I can't wait to never hear about him." Kate huffs, turns back to the mirror, picks up an eyelash curler from the jumble of beauty products heaped on the floor and begins curling her eyelashes.

"Just some motherly advice: you're actually supposed to curl your lashes before applying mascara."

"Thanks for being so open and honest about mascara." She stands up, walks over, snatches Tootles out of your arms, sets him on her desk, says nothing.

"I just need to know you're safe and—"

"God, Mom, just stop!" She pulls a black sweater out from under you without asking you to move.

Then someone knocking on your front door. Not a normal knock, knock, but an annoying knock-nuh-nuh-knock-knock. Jerry.

"I take it you don't need a ride," you say, as you follow her down the stairs. Kate opens the door for her ex-stepfather, and to your surprise, Miss Food Network follows him into your living room.

"Hi, Carrie."

You try to make your mouth work while Miss Food Network, who will certainly be cooking up some complicated, fancy-pants dinner like pasta with homemade sauce, strips off her coat and plops it down on the sofa. You didn't realize she'd be staying long enough to necessitate the removal of outerwear. At least this gives you a clear view of her stomach. Flatter than Kate's.

"Introductions! Carrie this is Svetlana. Svetlana, Carrie."

It would be sacrilege for her name to be anything other than Svetlana. You curse your mother for not naming you something exotic. Your tongue still out of commission, you reach out to shake. Svetlana hesitates for a moment, possibly examining your hand for signs of rabies or avian flu, then gives you her limp hand in return. You resent having to do all the work.

"Lana insisted on coming in to see where I used to live." Jerry seems unfazed by this.

Predictably, Poncho waddles his way into the meet-and-greet.

"Oooo, who is this little kitty?" Svetlana could not be bothered to give you a proper handshake but Poncho gets a full-on rubdown. Her use of the word "little" confirms your suspicions about her lack of good judgment.

"Do you guys want something to drink?" Kate asks, suddenly all smiles and manners. Jerry also takes it upon himself to remove his coat and throws it onto your couch. How did you forfeit your right to decide if and when layers of clothing were to be taken off and flung onto your furniture?

You ask Kate to please make your drink strong.

"Do you have Perrier?" Svetlana asks, to which Jerry adds that he'd like one as well. Then he takes her by the hand over to the loveseat, where they seat themselves. On the loveseat. He puts his hand on her thigh, her shoulder in his armpit. On the loveseat.

"Sorry, Mom only drinks Diet Mountain Dew or anything alcoholic. We have tap water if you want." You wonder what your daughter has the nerve to say when you're not around.

"Tap water will be fine, Kate. Lana, would you like a tour?" Really? Jerry wants to show his new girlfriend where he used to sleep with his ex-wife and where she now sleeps with her new boyfriend/fiancé who looks strikingly similar to her ex-husband? Svetlana, again displaying overt warning signs of bad judgment, claps her hands together in excitement about the tour... until she eyes something along the baseboard.

"What is *that*?!" she asks, drawing her knees up to her chest. Great, now her shoes are on your loveseat. She points at the mousetrap baited with a dollop of peanut butter in the corner of the living room. If you had known you would be entertaining company this afternoon you would've cleaned up. Maybe also moved the pile of laundry Ben folded, with your bras and underwear on top, from the chair in the living room to your dresser drawers. Maybe. But definitely hiding the mouse traps would've been a priority.

"Oh, the mousetrap... Well, I guess the fact that it doesn't have a rotting mouse carcass snapped inside is a good sign," you offer, "although it might be a bad sign—I think they're learning from each other's mistakes—I wouldn't leave your purse open or you might have to adopt a new pet." She wrinkles her nose and perches herself on the very edge of the loveseat, one hand grasping Jerry's closest knee, no doubt contemplating exit strategies should an army of mice come marching in through the vents.

Fact: Mice yearly kill an estimated three people worldwide.

Fact: Eastern European blondes yearly kill an estimated thirty people worldwide.

"I guess I should congratulate you in person," Jerry says, changing the subject from your squalid living conditions. You shake your head vigourously in response. A bobby pin flies across the room. You don't remember putting a bobby pin in your hair today.

"Sounds like you're going to have quite the wedding," Jerry continues just as Kate enters the room, carrying a glass in each hand. Thankfully, she appears not to have heard or else assumes Jerry was referring to someone else's wedding, most likely his own. Svetlana takes her glass from Kate and you notice she doesn't take even a small sip before placing it down on your coffee table without a coaster. You don't actually own coasters, but you at least would've expected her to use a magazine or one of Ben's students' tests, the way you do.

Jerry, however, happily consumes his tap water, contaminants and all. So happy in fact he decides to announce a toast as soon as Kate returns with the next two glasses and slams yours down on the side table next to you. You can't think of words fast enough so wave your arms like you've just gotten a bingo, your wings flapping in the windless living room.

"To the happy couple, Carrie and Ben, on their engagement!"

Kate looks at you, then at Jerry. You again, Jerry again. Then she walks to the centre of the living room, brings her glass high above her head, and smashes it down on the wooden floor. Poncho leaps from his nap; you think you hear a mouse squeak.

Game Over.
Sorry, you lose.
There are no more legal moves.
Do you want to play again?
Y/N?

Achieving Closure or
Alternatively Punching Anyone
in the Throat Who Tells You That
You Need Closure But When You
Ask What Closure Means They
React as if You've Just Asked
Them to Explain the Concept of
Colour to a Blind Person

- -

Things To Do
— End sham-engagement with Ben
— Visit mother's grave, bring two Crème Brûlée-flavoured
coffees so you can "pour one out"
— Plan trip to Disney World (how close to Pensacola?)
— Have talk with Kate (re: her father) (Google him first?)

— Have other talk with Kate (re: safe sex or taking a mother-daughter vow to swear off men for a period of at least four years or transferring her to an all-girls boarding school in the Northwest Territories, somewhere too cold to get undressed, ever)
— Find and keep boring day job
— Quit smoking
— Finish self-help book
— Let yourself feel one honest thing

- -

How to Quit Smoking
By: Carrie Fowler

1. Go cold turkey. Literally. Try replacing cigarettes with turkey cold cuts. If you are a vegetarian, try going cold Tofurky.

2. Try to eliminate as much stress as possible. Some ideas: take a break from taking a break from work, put wedding planning on hold, spend less time with your family, avoid stressful places like churches, gyms, tanning salons, and raw food restaurants.

3. Identify your smoking triggers. If, for instance, you enjoy smoking while drinking, cut back on the amount of time you spend drinking one-handed. Instead, try to always keep a drink in each hand, drinking simultaneously. You will lack both the time and the hand space required to smoke—and, soon, also the hand-eye coordination.

4. Keep your hands occupied with other tasks: bathing your cat, for example, requires all hands on deck. So do card games (you should be charging extra for puns like these, but you're not, mainly because you're not charging anything because you're not being paid to write this). If you have already mastered Step 3, then hooray for you, your hands are already occupied, or you have passed out under your kitchen table, but the important thing is that you aren't currently smoking. If you are a one-handed individual, bathing a cat or drinking with two hands is not recommended. One-handed drinking should suffice. If you are a no-handed individual, you have probably devised some genius way to smoke without the use of hands. Please do not tell how to do it. The author's doing quite well here with two piña coladas.

5. Book the longest trans-Pacific flight you can find. Tell the attractive person sitting next to you that for the next twelve hours he/she will have to be your anti-drug. Add a level of intrigue by not revealing which drug.

6. Get a new hobby. Something you can really pour yourself into, like compulsive gambling, obsessive online shopping, or pathological overeating.

7. When all else fails, try the nicotine gum. When you are addicted to the nicotine gum, revisit this helpful list.

- -

Perhaps it is all your fault, even though you had no other options. Ben did not exactly high-five you when you told him you had only accidentally proposed and had never intended a surprise Disney World wedding. He did, however, claim to have known all along and only meant to call your bluff (your sister also claims to have known from the beginning—apparently Disney World does not actually have a Snow White's Cottage and she was just "messing with you" [her words]).

The lies that were holding your relationship together begin unspooling faster than Poncho with a roll of toilet paper.

"And I know you haven't had a job for weeks," Ben says to you. He asked you to come sit with him at the kitchen table and when you took a seat, he put a cup of steaming herbal tea in front of you—either chamomile or grass-flavoured, you couldn't be certain. "I thought if I made up some story about quitting my job, you'd finally crack. I'd beat you at your own game. Quit teaching math to pursue art? C'mon, Carrie. What would I draw? Dodecahedrons? Heptahedron?"

"Hey, if you want to draw dinosaurs, I won't stop you."

"They're polyhedra."

"If you say so—I sure don't know anything about dinosaurs."

It happens so quietly, so smoothly, you don't even realize you've ended your relationship until it's done and Ben says, "I guess I better go."

He stands, pushes in his chair, leaves his mug of half-drunk tea on the placemat. He doesn't take anything with him, says he'll be back for it, but he has to get out of here, right now. He slips into his shoes by the backdoor, throws his jacket over one arm, and closes the door softly behind him before you can ask where he's going.

After that, you had to box all Ben's clothes and books and antique radios and store them on the front lawn until he could come claim them. Certainly no one expected you to sit quietly in the corner with your hands in your lap, watching him meticulously fold each argyle sweater and pack each of his six radios in bubble wrap and quadruple-check every drawer. You certainly didn't ask for rain thirty minutes after arranging everything he owned on the lawn; it hardly ever rains in Calgary.

- -

Things For Which You Are Proud of Yourself

1. You did not urinate on Splash Mountain or any other of the terrifying rides at Disney World with Kate last week.

2. Twenty minutes into the hour-long line for It's A Small World, fenced in by a family wearing matching droopy-eared Goofy hats to the front and a family passing the time by listing all the Disney movies they own on VHS in chronological order of release date to the rear, trapped to the right and left by metal guardrails, with nowhere to escape but into the sweaty, sticky sea of strange bodies, you forced her to have THE TALK.

3. Kate refused to say anything but "Shut up, Mom, stop being gross" for the rest of your forty minute wait, but when you were finally seated, all arms and legs inside the gondola, sailing slowly through a pastel two-dimensional representation of a yodeling Bavarian country, she turned to you and hissed "I'm not having sex, okay?"

Amid the snake-charmers and flying carpets of the Middle East, she whispered, barely audible over the theme song, that whenever she does start, she'll be safe, you don't have to worry. In a Hawaii that is depicted as being roughly the same size as the entire continent of Africa, she turned to you, said, "I'm not dumb, I'm not going to get pregnant like you did."

4. Another bonding moment occurred during your visit to Pensacola: after Tina's son bit your ankle totally unprovoked—how were you supposed to know the Fruit Roll-Ups were not grown-up food?—you became so overcome with gratitude you hadn't produce a son that you asked Kate if she wanted to braid each other's hair and paint each other's nails. She didn't. But still.

5. Next Monday you have a job interview at some company named after three old white guys, who are probably lawyers or accountants but you've avoided doing any research into the company so you can pretend they're a firm of freelance hitmen, which you will continue pretending to make the job more interesting should they happen to hire you.

6. You have successfully avoided picking Poncho up from Izzy who offered to pet-sit him while you vacationed in Florida—it has been five days since your return.

Izzy is also proud of you. She sees breaking off the engagement with Ben as a step forward in your grieving process.

You have come to realize that there are two types of people in this world: the type who actually like to make, and keep, appointments, who enjoy having their teeth cleaned and hair cut, who eagerly use up their employee health benefits on chiropractic appointments and orthopedic fittings, who would never say "I'm sure it'll go away on its own." And then there is the type for whom the thought of making small talk with the dental hygienist sends them into a blind panic; they've had an inexplicable chronic pain in their lower abdomen for weeks now, and while they do have health insurance, they'd rather "wait it out" than spend an hour at the clinic, and they're perfectly content with the kitchen-scissor haircut they've been giving themselves every month since their last appointment two Christmases ago. Perhaps unsurprisingly, your sister belongs to the former group. While Izzy has been seeing a psychiatrist for years, she recently added appointments with a hypnotist and a psychic to the line-up in an attempt to "unblock her subconscious."

"I have all these negative feelings about Mom and Dad I've been repressing for years," she tells you when she's at your house dropping off Poncho a week after you returned—Izzy stopped buying your excuses when you told her the house wasn't safe for Poncho to return to until you and Kate were cured of the contagious bout of beach foot you had contracted in Pensacola.

"You? What negative feelings could you possibly have?" you ask incredulously. Izzy had always been the favourite: earned good grades, followed the rules, didn't conceive a child one weekend in high school.

"Are you kidding?" she says, "Mom cried for a full forty-eight hours when I told her I was gay, and she spent the next decade implying I just hadn't found the right man yet. Do you know how many strange guys Mom had call me up and ask me on dates?" You honestly did not. You never imagined your mother and Izzy's relationship might be even more fucked-up than your own.

"You should see my shrink," she says, cycling through a two-inch-thick stack of business cards she's withdrawn from her wallet.

"Trust me, Iz, I'm repressing nothing." You assure her that you have no such blocks, your subconscious completely block-free.

"I'm as block-free as the unpopular kid in kindergarten."

"What?"

"Keep up. The other kids stole my blocks. That's how unpopular I am."

Still, she thinks you need to share your feelings.

"Do I have to share them with you?" you ask.

"Well, no, I guess not. Who do you want to share them with?"

"Twitter?"

"Carrie."

"You're right. It might be hard to actually come up with 140 characters. But actually, I'm working on a book. A self-help book."

"Ha."

"What?"

"You're being serious?"

"As serious as ovarian cancer. Actually, do you think that'd make a good title?"

"Who's this book for? Yourself?" Izzy asks, eyebrows up in her bangs.

*

When she leaves, you open a bag of baby carrots (your replacement for cigarettes because they're just like cigarettes, except not in any of the good ways) and your word processing document, read what you have written, highlight everything, and press the "delete" key. Poncho jumps onto the desk, waddles his way over to your computer, and plops himself onto your warm keyboard. Of course Poncho would have no faith in you to write anything. You shoo him off and then check to see how many letters have been permanently jammed into the keyboard and rendered unusable thanks to Poncho's thunderous weight. Your keyboard sustained no lasting damage. Shocking. Baby carrot, baby carrot. You check your email: a message from Izzy, begging you to be on time for your upcoming job interview, the time-stamp of which indicates she must have sent the email while she was still in your house. You stare at the white page. Baby carrot, baby carrot, baby carrot. Check your email again: no new messages in the last thirty seconds. Begin to type. One word. Two words. Baby carrot. A sentence. Baby carrot. Two sentences.

Tuesday your mother died. Ovarian cancer.

A Note From the Author

Dear Reader,

Thank you for buying this book. Due to its extremely limited print run, it is bound to become a collector's item and increase in value by at least 5-10%. If you are in possession of this book but you stole it, borrowed it from a friend, or found it at one of those free "take a book, leave a book" lending libraries, then please send an apology card full of money to my home address.

Congratulations on helping yourself become happy/rich/thin/in a relationship/a non-smoker/able to stay awake for a reasonable amount of time! You only have yourself to thank. Unless you were unsuccessful in changing your life. Then you only have yourself to blame. Please remember that I wrote the world's first true self-help book, so any negative feedback should be sent directly to yourself.

I hope this book was everything you hoped it would be and more. The "more" obviously referring to the pack of glittery scratch-and-sniff cat stickers included in every book. If you did not find any scratch-and-sniff cat stickers in this book, then either you stole, borrowed, or found this book—or my publisher unfathomably didn't go for the sticker idea.

One last thing: if you happen to recognize me on the street, please help me up.

Kisses,

Carrie

ACKNOWLEDGEMENTS

A huge thank you to Nicole Markotić for her editor-
ial expertise, guidance, and patience—and for cutting
approximately a thousand instances of the verb "to be."

Thank you to my grad school comrades and professors at
the University of Windsor and the University of Calgary,
where drafts of this novel were written, especially to
Janine Morris, Jess Nicol, Sandy Pool, Jonny Flieger, Rod
Moody-Corbett, Dale Jacobs, Louis Cabri, and Suzette Mayr.

I am also grateful to the Social Sciences and Humanities
Research Council and the University of Windsor for their
funding of this project.

A special mushy, love-filled thanks to my parents and
grandparents.

And finally to Brian Jansen. For everything.

HOLLIE ADAMS is a Windsorite living in Alberta, where she teaches writing and literature. She has studied creative writing at the University of Windsor and has a PhD in English from the University of Calgary. Her writing has been published in several Canadian periodicals including *Prairie Fire*, *The Antigonish Review*, *Carousel*, *The Windsor Review*, and *Filling Station*, and online at *McSweeney's Internet Tendency*.

Things You've Inherited From Your Mother
is her first novel.